The Rising Son

A Novel

Brian Kirk

ORIGINAL WRITING

© 2015 Brian Kirk

Cover image courtesy of the National Library of Ireland

All rights reserved. No part of this publication may be reproduced in any form or by any means—graphic, electronic or mechanical, including photocopying, recording, taping or information storage and retrieval systems—without the prior written permission of the author.

ISBNs
PARENT: 978-1-78237-996-6
EPUB: 978-1-78237-997-3
MOBI: 978-1-78237-998-0
PDF: 978-1-78237-999-7

A CIP catalogue for this book is available from the National Library.

Published by ORIGINAL WRITING LTD., Dublin, 2015.
Printed by ESSENTRA, Glasnevin, Dublin 11

For Martha and Ciarán

Acknowledgements

My thanks to The Arts Council of Ireland for a bursary received while writing the novel. I wish to acknowledge funding from South Dublin County Council's Commemorations Fund. I would also like to thank the following people for their valued support and advice: Laura Joyce, John Murphy, Tony Higgins, Nadene Ryan, Claire Hennessy and Dave Power.

Contents

Chapter 1	1
Chapter 2	7
Chapter 3	14
Chapter 4	23
Chapter 5	31
Chapter 6	40
Chapter 7	51
Chapter 8	56
Chapter 9	64
Chapter 10	73
Chapter 11	82
Chapter 12	90
Chapter 13	97
Chapter 14	105
Chapter 15	112
Chapter 16	119
Chapter 17	128
Chapter 18	135
Chapter 19	146
Chapter 20	155
Chapter 21	164
Chapter 22	171
Chapter 23	178
Chapter 24	183
Epilogue	192

Chapter 1

On the second night in his grandfather's house it all began. He was alone on a dark street, lit by occasional dim streetlights. There was a peculiar smell in the grey air, one that he could not name. In fact there was a mixture of smells; bad smells like the stench of farmyards for one, but many more besides. He was surprised to find that he was not afraid to be alone on this alien street. Part of him hoped that this was just a dream, but it felt more real than any dream he'd ever had before.

The street was empty, but in the distance he could hear a noise he thought might be thunder, or heavy barrels being rolled across cobblestones. He had the sense that the day had been hot, but now he felt the cool night air against his face and for a moment he thought of home. But it was just a word. He recognised the word, but he couldn't attach a place or memory to it in his mind. In fact he couldn't say where he was from, and in the same breath he realised he did not have a name. But once again the terror he should have felt at that moment was absent. In fact, he was barely there himself.

At the far end of the street he saw a figure approaching. It was a boy, roughly his own age. Jack was puzzled by the boy's bare feet and strange clothing; knee-length trousers, an old dark jacket that was too big for him, a cap and scarf. The year before his mother had taken him to see a production of Oliver in the West

End, and as he watched the boy, he thought of boys his own age acting the roles of Victorian child-villains.

'Howya! Are ye lost?'

He was so surprised when the boy spoke, he did not answer for a few moments. It was as if he was watching a play, not from the stalls as you normally would, but from the stage itself. But now the boy had burst the magic bubble; he had spoken to a member of the audience and the illusion was shattered.

'I'm... I suppose I am.'

The boy frowned.

'Are you English?'

'Yes, I mean, no – I suppose I'm Irish and English.'

'You can't be both these days – it's one or the other. Come along with me and I'll bring you where you're going. Where do you live?'

'I live with my grandfather, Michael O'Connor. It's number 52 Haroldville Avenue.'

'Shur that's only round the corner, I'll bring you there now. I'm Willie by the way.'

'Jack.'

His name came to him as if from a great distance and it comforted him that he had a name again, and that he had a new friend too. They shook hands formally like old men.

'Come on,' Willie said.

They set off walking, their footsteps echoing on the empty street.

'You must a left home in an awful hurry.'

'What do you mean?' Jack asked.

'Them clothes a yours. You must be frozen.'

Jack looked down and saw that he was wearing only a t-shirt and light pyjama trousers with slippers on his feet.

'Them shoes a yours look awful cosy but.'

'They are,' Jack said because he could think of nothing else to say to this strange boy.

They rounded the corner and Jack realised that they were now on his grandfather's street, but it looked different somehow. Perhaps it was just the darkness; the streetlights gave off so little light and there were no lights on in any of the neighbours' windows.

Suddenly there was a scattering of shouts at one end of the street and then a deafening high-pitched sound that seemed to echo off the fronts of the terraced houses – a kind of shrill zinging. The air was filled with a new smell now. It was smoke. Jack recognised it straight away because he'd walked past the remnants of a burnt out house with his stepfather on their way to see Arsenal play one Saturday. Both boys threw themselves on the ground instinctively and whatever light there was had now been extinguished. Jack reached out a hand to feel for Willie but felt only the damp cold stone of the road. He shut his eyes tight and opened them again, but there was only darkness. He heard heavy boots running, coming closer, a momentary pause and then more gunfire. He screamed.

He woke in a sweat. The bedclothes were on the floor and he was wrapped only in an old tartan blanket he'd found on top of the wardrobe the night before when he was cold and couldn't get to sleep. The room smelled of must and damp. There was another smell mixed in there too, he thought it could be smoke. He tried to open the window to let in some air but it was useless; it was painted shut – had been for years. Everything about this house was old and stuffy and reeked of the past.

The day before Jack's grandfather had taken him into town for a treat. Since his mother had abandoned him he had been quiet and surly. On the way home they rode the tram along the quays until they came to the museum where they walked around the exhibits, and all the while his grandfather provided a constant commentary.

'You must always remember Jack, that you are an Irish man. You may have been born in London and lived all your twelve years there, but you are as Irish as I am.'

Everything in the museum was old. That's the way it was with museums – he knew this from trips with his mother to the British Museum and Natural History Museum. But it wasn't just the museum; the whole city of Dublin seemed old to Jack – compared to London it was tired and small and enclosed, and the grey sky seemed to press down on the rooftops, trapping him, stopping him from being where he wanted to be, in London with his mother and his friends.

His Grandfather showed him the uniforms worn by British and Irish soldiers over the years, sometimes taking the time to read aloud from the information provided on panels beside the exhibits.

'This is where we all come from Jack. It's our history. Do you see?' Grandad looked at the boy.

He was wasting his breath, Jack thought. There was no point to this. It was all in the past. That's what history was – even he knew that. The past was no good to him. At best it was a distraction from the present. It was the future that worried Jack.

When he thought about the future he could feel his heartbeat race inside his chest and his head would grow light. His mother told him it was just a holiday, that she would be back to get him in a couple of weeks. She had some things to see to, that was all. He was a child, but he was not a fool. She was trying to patch things up with Matt, he knew that. His stepfather had left them a month before. For weeks before that Jack had stood on the landing at night and listened to them arguing. He didn't know what the cause of their arguments was but he assumed, as children do, that it was his fault. Perhaps Matt didn't want him; he wanted a boy of his own – he had said that before – but that was never going to happen, Mum said.

Matt wasn't bad. He had always been good to Jack, and Jack had no expectation of him beyond the things he did for him. He took him to football or cricket practise, he made fried breakfasts on Saturdays and brought him to the Emirates Stadium to see Arsenal play; he called him mate and bought him ice-creams and football magazines. Jack was happy enough with that. But Matt wanted more – that was why he had said on one of those nights when they argued just before he moved out:

'I want a child of my own, Kate – what's so wrong with that?'

Jack took deep breaths and put his hand against his heart to feel the pulse quicken as he listened from the landing above.

Was Matt more important to his mother than he was? That was the question he was trying not to ask himself since he came here. When she said goodbye to him she hurried out the door. Her taxi was waiting, and she had a plane to catch. And when she was gone he looked at this old man, this stranger – his grandfather supposedly – and sensed that the old man was looking back at him and thinking the exact same thing.

His mother spoiled him. She indulged him. He came first, he always had done and Jack had grown accustomed to that. Something had changed somehow, but she was not about to tell him what that was or maybe she felt he was too young to understand. But he was not too young. In the absence of hard facts he feared the worst. Perhaps she didn't want him anymore.

Now as they stood before an original copy of the Proclamation of the Irish Republic, Jack tried to listen to his grandfather's commentary, but it was useless. He was thinking about his mother, and about Matt, and what they might be saying at that very moment to each other about him.

'Is Matt Irish, Grandad?'

'No, Jack, he's English.'

'Is that why he and Mum can't be together?'

Grandad laughed briefly, but stopped when he noticed Jack's frowning face.

'No. No. That has nothing to do with anything. Sometimes people disagree over things. It's complicated, that's all. You'll understand when you're older.'

The old man placed his hand gently on Jack's head and ruffled his unruly dark hair. Why did everyone treat him like a baby?

Chapter 2

The following morning Jack couldn't get out of bed. He was so tired. He felt like he had not slept at all. Had it really been a dream or had he actually been wandering the city for half the night with a new friend? He wondered how Willie was, or where he was. He could hear his grandfather's gruff voice calling him from the kitchen downstairs, but he just lay there and thought how ridiculous Grandad's Irish accent sounded.

That first day, after his mother went back to London, he hardly understood a word the old man said, but he did not bother asking him to repeat himself. The truth was he was a little bit afraid of his mother's father. He did not always shave and his clothes looked old and worn. The sweater that he wore to the museum had a hole under the left armpit, but he did not seem to notice, or if he did, to care. Jack stood off a little way from him on the tram, not wanting to be seen with such a scruffy man.

And now he was shouting at him.

'Jack O'Connor! Get up now out a that! You're wasting the best part of the day. Don't make me go up there and drag you out of it!'

Jack shivered at the thought of his grandfather pulling him from the bed.

'Come on Jack! Your cornflakes are going cold!'

That was just nonsense. How could cornflakes go cold? Unless... Oh God, no! Not hot milk – anything but that. That burnt nutty taste, and the slimy skin that always formed on it.

Jack pulled on his tracksuit bottoms and raced downstairs.

'Ah there you are! I thought you were dead in the bed.'

Jack sat at the table in front of a bowl of cornflakes. He was relieved to see that the milk had not yet been poured.

'You'll have tea?' Grandad said, filling a large mug for him.

'I don't like tea.'

'What do ya mean? We O'Connors were reared on tea.'

'I don't like the taste. Mum never gives it to me.'

Jack could see his grandfather scowl when he used the word mum.

'I don't know what your *mam* does be thinking half the time.'

After breakfast Jack excused himself while the old man settled down with the newspaper to study the racing pages.

'Don't go too far now,' he warned without lifting his eyes from the page.

The street was quiet, a narrow street of terraced Victorian two-bed houses with no front gardens and tiny yard space at the rear. Jack saw a man across the street who seemed to be watching him, but he could not be sure. He was young with longish hair and he looked a bit familiar. At one point Jack thought he was going to cross the road to speak to him, but then he turned away and took his phone from his pocket and studied it closely as if he had received a very important message.

Jack remembered his dream clearly now and he noticed how different the street looked in real life even though the houses were exactly the same. It was the cars. He realised that there had been no cars at all in his dream. Now there were cars parked all along one side of the road, leaving just enough room for others to pass up and down.

He walked to the end of the road and turned the way he'd come from in his dream. It was another, wider, street lined with slightly larger houses, just as he remembered it from the previous night. As he walked he tried to make sense of the fact that he was now seeing this street for the first time, but recognising it also as the same street he had walked down the night before in his dream. How could that be? There must be some sort of explanation. He walked on for a while longer until it struck him that he must have actually seen the street before, when his mother brought him here a few days ago. He probably just remembered it without having consciously noted it in the first place. Yes, that must be it! The human brain can do amazing things – his mother and Matt had often talked about stuff like that. They worked in advertising and knew about these things. *Subliminal*, that's what they'd called it.

When he reached the top of the road he thought he saw the young man watching him again.

'Watch where you're going youngfella!'

Distracted, Jack had walked straight into a boy on a bicycle. The boy braked hard and jack-knifed the bike so that the front wheel struck Jack on the knee.

'Oh sorry!' Jack cried, as his hand moved to the source of the pain.

'Just watch it in future!' the boy warned. He was older than Jack, by a year or two perhaps, but not much bigger.

'You shouldn't be cycling on the path, you know.' Jack didn't like the look of the boy and was upset by the pain he felt, but he was also annoyed at himself for the way he had so quickly apologised.

'What did you say?' The boy had been on the point of cycling away but now he stopped and turned the bike towards Jack again.

'I said, you shouldn't be cycling on the path, that's all.'

'Here, are you English or something?'

'No, I'm Irish. I'm as Irish as you are.'

'Well you don't sound like it to me. This is my country and I'll cycle where I want – okay?'

'I was just saying.'

'Yeah well don't, not unless you want to wake up with a crowd around you!'

Jack turned away.

'Hey come here!' The boy beckoned him now, a lop-sided smile breaking across his face.

'Yeah?'

'Why aren't you at school?' the boy asked.

'I don't live here – I'm on holiday I suppose.'

'Okay.'

'So why aren't you at school?'

'Who says I'm not?' The boy winked. 'Hey, do you want to see something cool?'

'What is it?

'It's a surprise. Come on, it's not far.'

'I have to go home soon.' Jack's natural curiosity was tempered by his fear of his grandfather.

'Okay then, it's your loss bud!' The boy placed his right foot on the raised pedal, showing his clear intention to leave.

'If we're really quick I can go I suppose.'

'We'll be no time at all – come on!'

Jack ran alongside the boy as he cycled along the South Circular Road. Soon they came to a busy junction where traffic lights held back lines of cars and buses. The boy moved skilfully between the traffic and Jack knew as he followed that his mother would have killed him if she could have seen him.

On the far side of the road there was a huge church. Churches were everywhere in this city and they all looked the same to him: bleak and grey and uninviting. Jack was surprised when the boy swung in through the open gate and pedalled across the smooth tarmac of the car park towards the rear. At the back of the church there was a kind of shrine with a statue of the Virgin Mary mounted on a rock behind a wrought iron fence. Another, older, boy, was standing by the fence and he turned and smiled when he saw them approach.

Jack remembered Matt teasing his mother about moving statues in Ireland once before and now he wondered was this statue one of those. Was he going to see a plaster statue suddenly turn and look at him or point at him? He wasn't sure he wanted to see that kind of thing at all, and he began to regret agreeing to come along.

He stopped a little way off and thought about running away. Why should he care what these boys thought of him? He would probably never see either of them again. But he couldn't do it. He just stood there until the two boys approached him.

'So you're English?' the older one said. He was ugly, skinny with blond hair that was shaved at the sides. He wasn't much taller than the boy on the bike but up close Jack could see he was actually much older. Blond bristles grew in patches around fiery acne volcanoes on his cheeks and along his jaw line.

'I'm Irish, I told you,' Jack said to the one who had been on the bicycle.

'You don't sound like it,' Ugly said. He turned to his friend. 'He doesn't sound Irish, does he?'

Biker shook his head slowly.

'I should really be going,' Jack said.

'But you haven't had your surprise yet.'

'It's alright, I've changed my mind. I need to go back now. My grandad will be looking for me.'

The two boys looked at each other and laughed as if Jack had said something amusing.

Ugly stepped forward now and grabbed Jack by his arms. His breath stank of smoke.

'Hold still, will ya! We're just checking your pockets.'

'Jesus, he has nothing! Have you no money at all?'

'No I don't.'

'Here what's this? Bloody football cards, and worse – they're all Arsenal!'

'Arse-nil is right!' Biker sneered.

Ugly held him tighter from behind and Biker punched him hard in the stomach. Jack thought he might be sick.

They laughed again and Ugly let him go for a moment, but then he got serious again and stood in front of Jack, almost standing on his toes and staring down into his face.

'You come back here tomorrow okay? Bring some money this time, at least twenty euro, and then we'll show you something you won't forget.'

He pushed Jack away roughly.

'Off you go now. And remember – tomorrow at the same time. We'll be watching you!' He held the tips of two splayed fingers to his eyes and then pointed them at Jack.

'Brits out!' Biker shouted after him as he rounded the side of the church, and in the distance Jack could hear them laughing.

Chapter 3

Later that evening Jack's mother phoned. Jack watched as his grandfather held the receiver silently to his ear. He could hear a tinny, indistinct version of his mother's voice, but could not make out what she was saying. He tried to engross himself in FIFA on his DS, but the old man's grunted replies made it impossible for him to concentrate.

He didn't mention the incident with Biker and Ugly when he got home earlier. He went straight to his room and lay on the bed wishing he could be back at home in Islington, far away from this strange and scary place. He thought about how weird Dublin was. It looked a bit like London, and the people looked the same too – they even spoke the same language, but it was definitely different. It was as if reality was skewed here, the way it was in dreams, the way it had been in that peculiar dream he had the previous night – it seemed like the real world, but it wasn't and it made him feel weird.

Grandad was holding the phone out to him.

'It's your mam, she wants to talk to you.'

Part of him wished he could be hard enough to say no, that she was the last person he wanted to speak to right now. But he couldn't do it. He longed to hear her voice again, and more than anything he hoped that she was calling to say that she was coming soon to get him.

'Jack, love, how are you?'

'Fine.'

He was disappointed by the curt tone of his voice. Why did he do that?

'Is everything okay there? Are you having a nice time with Grandad?'

Jack did his best to fight the hurt that he felt welling up inside him. She knew how he felt about being here, so why did she persist in this pretence, acting as if this was some kind of holiday? He had been dumped here without being given any say. He could have stayed with his friend Jason and not missed out on school or football matches, but instead she suddenly decided to leave him with her father, a man she hardly ever talked about and rarely ever called.

'I... I'm fine,' he lied. He couldn't tell her the truth about how he felt with the old man listening to every word he said.

'Dad is so pleased to have you there. He's been telling me all the things you've been doing.'

'When are you coming to collect me?'

There was a short but telling silence on the line.

'I just need a little more time Jack. It won't be long though.'

Jack knew she was lying. All the animation drained out of her voice when she spoke, as if she couldn't force herself to dramatise the lie he knew it was.

'I love you Jack.'

Why did she have to say that? Tears burned behind his eyes, but he would not let them show, not with the old man there to see them. Deep down he wanted to say something comforting to her, something that would tell her that of course he loved her, but something that would also make it clear to her that he was not happy here.

'I miss London,' was all that he could manage. 'I'm sure I'm missing out on stuff at school and there are football trials as well.' His voice trailed off. He knew he sounded selfish.

'I know, Jack, I'm sorry. Things will be back to normal soon.'

He wished he could believe her. But she sounded worn out, exhausted by the effort of lying to him perhaps. For a second he thought about asking her directly why he couldn't be with her, but he was afraid of what she might say. The more he thought about it, the more he sensed that Matt was not the true reason she had left him there.

Dinner was meat and potatoes again. That was all his grandfather seemed to be able to cook. One day he'd opened a tin of beans for breakfast and Jack considered that a treat. Most of the time it was bacon or sausages or chops and always with potatoes. They'd sat all afternoon watching the racing on TV, the old man drinking endless cups of tea while Jack worried about where he was going to get the twenty euro for Ugly and Biker the following morning.

That night when the house was quiet and the old man was asleep Jack crept downstairs to the kitchen. He looked in all the cupboards, opening boxes and tins, hoping to find some money hidden somewhere around the place. But there was nothing.

He went back up to his room and lay awake, worried, breathing in the smell of must and damp. Each time he closed his eyes he saw their faces: Biker winking, Ugly sneering.

After a while Grandad put his head around the door.

'Are you having trouble sleeping Jack?'

Jack sat up quickly in the bed.

'If I didn't know better I'd say you had a guilty conscience – would I be right at all?'

'I can't get comfortable, that's all.'

'What were you looking for downstairs?'

'Nothing. I just needed to stretch my legs.'

'And open every press in the house too?'

Jack's mouth opened wide. 'I wasn't… I wasn't…'

'You were looking for something, weren't you?'

'Yes.' Jack's mind raced, trying to think of something harmless he might say.

'Was it money?'

'Yes.' God, he was an idiot. If only he'd said anything else but that.

Grandad put his hand in his dressing gown pocket and took out a roll of crisp euro notes.

'Your mam left this with me for you, but I believe a man should be able to look after his own finances, don't you?'

Jack nodded.

He handed the notes to Jack.

'Where did you find this?' Grandad lifted the old tartan blanket from the bed.

'It was on top of the wardrobe – I was cold last night,' Jack said.

Grandad held the blanket briefly to his face and then folded it carefully. He looked sad.

'I'm sorry Grandad, I didn't mean to…'

'No, no, no, I'm not cross.' Grandad smiled. 'It was your grandmother's. I just haven't seen it for a while, that's all.'

Grandad reached up and put the blanket back on top of the wardrobe.

'I'll leave you,' he said. 'Try to sleep now. I always try to remember happy things; that always gets me off to sleep. Goodnight now Jack.

'Goodnight Grandad.'

He thought that he might dream about Willie again. He hoped he might find him because he was worried about how the dream had ended, the gunfire and the darkness all around them. With the money safely tucked away into his bedside locker, he no longer worried about the prospect of seeing Ugly and Biker the next day, and tiredness overcame him. He fell into a deep sleep almost immediately. But he did not dream.

The following morning he got up before Grandad had to give him a second call. After breakfast he went upstairs and took a twenty euro note from the locker and put it in his pocket. The old man had settled himself at the table with the racing page and pen and paper as he had the day before.

'I'm just going for a walk Grandad.'

'Okay, Jack, but be careful. Don't go too far.' Again he didn't raise his eyes from the page.

Jack had the feeling that his Grandad probably didn't want him either. After all, he had his own life, his own set of idle routines, and Jack most likely was just a tedious distraction from what the old man wanted to be doing.

Outside it was cool; it was still only April. He made his way along the street, thinking about Willie and wondering who he was and how he had conjured him so clearly in his dream. He soon found himself at the busy junction and he dutifully waited for the lights to change before he stepped out on the road. There was something on in the church today. Lines of older people in ones and twos made their way across the car park to the main door at the front. One or two looked at him and smiled as he turned in the gate with them.

He was relieved when he came around the side of the church and saw that no one was about. He walked up to the grotto where the statue of Mary stood, her head perpetually tilted, her hands joined in prayer. His mother never brought him to mass, never had him baptised even. He didn't get any of it; the praying, the bowing, the kneeling. He put his hand in his jeans pocket and felt the smooth edge of the twenty note. Better he kept the money anyhow than let those two have it.

'So you came? I thought you'd be a no show to be honest.'

It was Biker. He appeared behind Jack suddenly, probably emerging from the side door of the church.

Jack considered for a moment if he could hold his own if it came down to a fight. Biker was only a little taller, but he was strong. Jack remembered the force of the punch he'd taken in the stomach the day before.

'So let's see your money then?'

'I haven't got it,' Jack said.

Biker laughed.

'Course you have it – you wouldn't be here if you didn't.'

Jack was peculiarly impressed by Biker's logic.

'Maybe I do have it,' he said.

'Here Paddy Englishman, I don't have time for this – just pay up now or face the consequences!'

'No, I'm not paying. I'm going home now.'

Biker smiled at him.

'I was hoping you'd say that.' He put two fingers in his mouth and emitted a loud whistle.

Ugly and two other boys emerged from the side door of the church.

'Bet you wish you'd paid up now, eh?' Biker sneered.

'Here, here, take it – look I have it here. It's all I have!' Jack was panicking now as the others approached.

'Sorry bud, it's too late now, so it is. You had your chance, but you wanted to play the hard man, so you might as well give it a shot. Come on now!'

The boys were right on top of him by now and Jack closed his eyes and placed his hands across his cowering head. Already he could feel the force of the blows he was about to receive. But nothing happened. He heard a scurrying of boots and hoarse shouts and opened his eyes to find his Grandad holding Ugly by the ear. The others had all fled.

'Don't let me catch you fellas near my grandson again or I'll come looking for you! Do you hear me?' He twisted Ugly's already enlarged ear even more.

'Do you hear me, I said?'

'Yes, yes. Please let me go!' The older boy was almost crying. Jack tried not to look at him. He was impressed by Grandad's strength.

The old man let him go eventually and Ugly raced away, rubbing an inflamed ear, only to stop when he was a safe distance away.

'You better watch yourself mister – I know where you live! We'll come and get you back for this!'

'Go on outa that ya pup!' Grandad shouted and made as though to chase him, but Ugly took no chances and ran off to join his gang.

'Did they get your money Jack?'

'No.' Jack still had the note clenched tightly in his fist.

'Maybe I should take it just to be on the safe side.'

Jack gave him the note.

On the way back home neither one spoke, but when they got inside Grandad put on the kettle and made a pot of tea while Jack sat at the kitchen table. Grandad filled two mugs and added extra milk to Jack's, before taking the sugar bowl down from the shelf and putting two spoonfuls in both mugs and stirring them well. This time Jack tasted the tea. It felt hot on his tongue which was nice, and sweet too, in a way he had not expected. He finished every drop.

Grandad smiled at him.

'Now you're a real O'Connor.'

Jack smiled.

'Thanks Grandad.'

'For what?'

'Just thanks for everything. I'm sorry I haven't been very nice to you since I got here. I just missed my mum and my friends.'

'That's alright Jack. It's only natural. I know it was hard to come here, to live with an old man that you don't really know. But I'm your Grandad, and that matters – blood is thicker than water as they say.'

'I don't understand what that means.'

'It just means we're family, and family comes before everyone else in this world because they're the ones who love you the most.'

'The way Mum loves me more than Matt does?'

'She's your mother Jack; no one could love you more.'

Jack said nothing. He looked at the floor.

'And she's my daughter,' Grandad said.

Jack looked up at the old man. Grandad looked a little uncomfortable.

'How come you never visited us in London, Grandad?' he asked.

Grandad scowled. That was the kind of expression that had scared Jack a little when he first arrived. But after a moment his features softened and he smiled at his grandson.

'The past is hard to explain sometimes. I think what we need now, Jack, is a little history lesson.'

Chapter 4

That afternoon Grandad took Jack to the Phoenix Park for a walk. The park was beautiful; the leaves beginning to show already on most of the trees and the grass lush and green. It was as if they had momentarily stepped outside the city and were walking deep in the countryside. The old man led him away from the traffic on the main road across the playing fields, and Jack pretended he was in a new country far away from Dublin, where the sky was permanently blue and anything was possible.

'You know your mam loves you very much Jack, don't you?' Grandad said.

Jack wished he had not spoken. It brought him back to the real world with a bump.

'I know,' he said.

'She just needs a bit of time for herself right now. You understand, don't you?'

'It has to do with Matt, doesn't it?' Jack asked.

'A bit I suppose, but you shouldn't worry. Sometimes grown-ups need a little time to think things out. Anyway, I'm happy that you came to visit me. I'm sorry that you never came before.'

Grandad looked away towards the huge cross that stood in the distance before turning in that direction and striding off ahead of Jack.

'Why did you never come to visit us, Grandad?' Jack asked, jogging to keep up.

For a moment he thought the old man was not going to answer. But after a few more paces he stopped and looked down at Jack. While he no longer found him frightening, Jack sensed something unsettling in his demeanour.

'Families are funny Jack,' he said. 'I wasn't always the best father in the world. Your mother and I, we fell out – years ago – long before you were born. You take so much for granted...' He began, but stopped, and his brow creased, frustrated by his inability to find the right words to express his complicated thoughts. 'Things I thought were black and white turned out not to be. There's always some grey in the picture I've learned.'

Jack had no idea what the old man was talking about, but he said nothing and they both set off walking again, a little slower now.

'You see that cross there?'

'Yeah.' You'd have to be blind not to, Jack thought.

'Well they built that for when the Pope came in 1979. He said mass out here in the park and people came from all over the country to see him. Over a million people came. I was there with your grandmother – God rest her – and your mam. It was a great day.'

Jack couldn't imagine his mother being at mass here in a field, or at any mass for that matter. He tried to figure out what age she must have been back then. She was forty-four now so that made her... He thought about it for a moment – he enjoyed mental maths. Seven! That's it, she was seven. He wondered did she remember it and made a mental note to ask her about it when he saw her next. Then he felt a pang of loneliness, as if she was gone forever, but he told himself that he was being silly, just feeling sorry for himself.

'I remember that day so well. It was September, but the sun was splitting the stones. We brought fold-up chairs and a picnic and we sang along with the hymns. Everyone was in a great mood. I really believed that the Pope had brought something new, something good to our poor country. Times were hard then. I'd just lost one job and it took me a while to find another, but I felt hopeful that day. That's what I remember most of all.'

'Did the Pope find a new job for you?' Jack asked.

Grandad laughed.

'No son, no. Or maybe he did, who knows. But I got a lot out of that day at the time. It's hard to explain.'

Jack could see cars parked near the cross as they approached; they looked tiny, like kids' toys. He wasn't sure what to say. Grandad seemed to be miles away, reliving that day in his mind.

'What was Grandma like?' Jack asked.

That brought a smile to Grandad's face.

'Ah she would have loved to hear you ask that, Jack. Poor Angela, God rest her. She was a lovely woman, beautiful, and smart too – just like your mam. Twenty-four years she's gone, but I still feel as if she's with me every day. Do you find that hard to believe?'

Jack shook his head.

'That blanket in your room – Angela got it as a wedding present years ago from some old aunt who doted on her. She said it was a special blanket. I think she really believed it would make her better.'

'But it didn't, did it Grandad?'

'No son. She died just months before your mother moved to London.'

'She must have been very young.'

'She was. Forty-five.'

'That's just one year older than Mum is now,' Jack said.

Jack thought of his mother then and felt sad again.

'How did she die Grandad?'

'It was a thing called Huntington's disease, son. There's no cure for it. She just got weaker and weaker over time. It was awful. She was too young to go, but by the end she was suffering so much…'

Jack had never heard of that disease before. Part of him wanted to know more, but he did not want to upset Granddad. He was impressed with Grandad and how he had been able to talk about his wife's illness without fear in his voice. He looked up at the old man. His mouth felt dry and he thought he might cry.

'Those whom the gods love…' Grandad began, but he couldn't finish.

'Then you were on your own Grandad, after Mum left?'

'Yes.'

'You must have missed Mum so much when she went to London.'

'I did. I missed her every day.'

'But you kept in touch by phone and e-mail?'

Grandad stopped and looked at him.

'Well I didn't have a phone back then and e-mail wasn't invented yet – well, not around here anyway. I don't think I knew what a computer was back then.'

'So how did people keep in touch Grandad?'

'They sent letters.'

'Letters?'

'Yes, you know, letters in the post.'

'But that must have taken ages. How did you have a conversation?' Jack asked.

'You didn't really, I suppose.' Grandad was thoughtful for a moment. 'You told your news and they wrote back with their news. You couldn't really talk.'

'So that's how you and Mum kept in touch, by snail mail?'

'Yeah, it was hard.'

'It sounds like something out of an old story,' Jack said.

'It does, yes, I know. It's history, that's what it is. I said you needed to learn some history and this is it.'

Grandad sat on a bench across the road from the Papal Cross. He patted the seat beside him to indicate to Jack that he should sit down.

'Sometimes when I walk I get jumbled up in my thoughts. It must be my age,' he said. 'I'll be honest with you Jack. If we're to be friends we always have to tell each other the truth, even if we're not proud of some of the things we've done. When your mam left home we weren't even speaking. Things had happened at home, things I won't go into now, but it was hard enough with your grandmother dying and all. So when your mam went to London I lost contact with her for a while. I had no address for her for years.'

Jack stood up off the seat. He had an urge to run and keep on running until he got away from Grandad and the city and all the threats of the past, but he was afraid to move. He felt that he was all alone and had nowhere else to go. He wanted to run to meet his future in a place far away from here, a place where his mother and his friends were waiting for him. But since he came to Dublin he was confused between the past and future. He wanted to go back and forward at the same time; back to London, forward to the future he'd always imagined for himself there. But that prospect seemed to be consigned to the past already.

Jack didn't run away. He just decided to stop listening. He let the old man rattle on while he stared into space and nodded now and then.

That evening after they'd finished eating their tea the doorbell rang. Grandad had strange eating habits. He ate his dinner in the middle of the day and at dinner time he ate a meal that he called tea which usually involved brown bread and a boiled egg. Lunch was unheard of, but sometimes there was supper of chips from the local chippie – only Grandad called it the chipper.

By now Jack was feeling settled in so he went to answer the door. When he opened it he was surprised to see a boy of around his own age and an older girl standing in front of him. The boy was smiling broadly but the girl stared at him coldly. She finally said something that he could not understand, and so after a few moments of staring blankly at her, he called over his shoulder to Grandad to come out. He stepped inside the front room and listened, his heart pounding in his chest, as the girl spoke to his grandad.

'Mam says can you come and have a look at her radiators – they're not heating up again.'

She was a plain-spoken girl, but there was something in her confident tone that Jack was taken by.

'That's no bother at all Sally, I'll call in tomorrow morning. Tell your mother to have the kettle on.' Grandad laughed.

'I will Mr. O'Connor,' Sally said. 'Was that your grandson who opened the door?'

'Yes, that's Jack from London. He'll be with me for a while.'

'Mam says you're to be sure to bring him along too.'

Jack found it unbearable to stand just feet away while they talked about him in this way. He got up all his courage and came out to the door again.

'Ah, here he is, here's Jack now!' Grandad beamed at him. 'Say hello to Sally and Peadar, Jack.'

'Hello Sally. Hello Peadar.' Jack put out his hand and Sally took it firmly in hers.

'He's very posh, isn't he, Mr. O'Connor?' She said to Grandad, ignoring Jack.

Grandad laughed.

'Oh he is that alright! Just like meself.'

The three of them shared a laugh while Jack just stood there red-faced, staring at Sally.

Peadar reached out and took his hand now and shook it roughly.

'Very pleased to meet you, Jack,' he said as he smiled.

Jack shook his hand. Peadar seemed to be peculiarly old-fashioned for his years.

'Do you play football at all?' Peadar asked.

'Yes, I do.'

'Great stuff! We'll have a kickabout tomorrow then.'

Jack nodded. He was still looking at Sally. She was maybe three years older than him, much taller, and she had shoulder length dark brown hair. Her skin was lightly freckled around the nose and her eyes were big and brown. When she laughed her full lips formed a perfect bow and little wrinkles formed around the edges of her eyes.

When she was gone Grandad simply said:

'Lovely girl that Sally Morrison.'

Jack wasn't sure if he was expected to reply so he said nothing. After a while he said goodnight and went up to his room. He lay awake in bed for a while, listening to the sounds of the city outside, trying to stop himself from thinking too much. He wished he could sleep. After a while he got up and took his grandmother's blanket down from the wardrobe where Grandad had left it. He wrapped it around himself and got back into bed. He shut his eyes and tried to picture his mother's face.

Chapter 5

His eyes were closed. He could feel warm sun on his face, a light breeze. All around him he heard the sound of people in motion, the bustle of a city beginning its day. But there was something missing also.

He opened his eyes and took in the scene around him. For that is what he thought it was; a scene from a film or a play. Men and women and children walked or rode bicycles, hurrying past, some of them giving him curious looks as they went. There were horses pulling light two-wheeled carts and, at the far end of the street, he saw what looked like an ancient car approaching, roofless with round-eyed front lights, making an awful racket. He looked down at his clothes and felt foolish when he realised he was wearing only pyjamas.

Jack knew immediately where he was. Although he did not recognise the street as his grandad's, he sensed that he was somewhere in the general neighbourhood. He watched the faces of the children that passed by, looking for Willie among them, but they all seemed better dressed, neater looking than he had been. Mothers reached out and held their offspring by the arm as they walked past him, shushing the questions of the younger ones as they went. He set off walking in the direction he hoped was home.

A bell clanged loudly behind him and a tram bearing the banner *Shaw's Sausages* passed slowly, full to bursting with people who appeared to be overdressed for the heat of the day. He stood on the pavement and watched as it passed and was almost hit by a boy passing on a bicycle. The boy shouted something over his shoulder as he continued on his way and Jack thought of Biker and Ugly and shuddered.

What was this place? It was Dublin certainly, but not as it should be. It was only a dream, he told himself. Soon he would be awake, lying in his bed in Grandad's house, breathing in the earthy smell of damp.

Then he saw him. It was definitely Willie, walking hurriedly on the far side of the road, a brown paper package tucked under his arm. Without thinking he ran to catch him up. He called his name.

'Willie! Willie!'

But Willie had turned down a road to the left and by the time Jack had made the turn he could see the boy being let into a house. He wasn't sure what to do next, so he waited outside for a while. He thought about knocking on the door, but he was worried about the impression he might make on Willie's parents – he assumed this was his home – what with his strange clothes and his foreign accent. He thought he saw the net curtains move and a head appear at an upstairs window, and he felt suddenly wounded, wondering had Willie heard him calling and simply chosen to ignore him.

He decided to go. He would ask the next person he met how to get to Haroldville Avenue, but there were far fewer people on this smaller street. He noticed how well the street looked in the bright sunshine, and he wondered again if this really could be Willie's house. The boy had looked poor, but this house was well kept and had large bay windows on the ground and upper floors.

No one was coming so he ambled back in the direction he had come from, turning every now and again to keep an eye out for Willie. He stopped at the top of the road and prepared what he would say to the first person who passed.

'Excuse me, could you tell me how to get to Haroldville Avenue please?'

'Such a polite boy!' A severe looking woman in a long, dark dress and matching hat grimaced at him. She turned to her companion, an older, worn looking woman dressed all in black.

'I blame the parents, you know, letting their offspring run riot all over the city.' She turned back to Jack. 'Is your father a soldier then?'

'No,' Jack replied. 'My father is dead.'

She turned to the old woman again.

'Ah, the war is a terrible thing, so it is.'

By now Jack was fed up with the woman – he just wanted directions.

'And your mother, where is she?'

'She's in London.'

'London? God help us!'

'I'm staying with my Grandfather on Haroldville Avenue, but I'm lost.'

'Oh, he's lost, the poor thing – did you hear that Mama?'

Something moved behind Jack then and he turned away from the women in just enough time to see Willie run full tilt across the road and away from him. Jack set off in pursuit once again without thinking.

'Hey you there! Boy! Come back here!'

Why was his new friend trying to get away from him? It made no sense. He ignored the exclamations of the startled woman and pumped his arms and legs as fast as he could go.

All the sport and football he played in school paid off. It wasn't long until Willie gave in; he turned down a side street and stopped, bent over gasping for air, hardly able to speak.

'What ... what do you want?'

'It's me Willie. It's me – don't you recognise me? It's Jack.'

Willie's breathing was returning to normal. The sun was behind Jack and Willie squinted suspiciously at him.

'How do you know my name?' he panted.

'We met the other night, Willie.'

The boy continued to stare at him.

'You're English,' he said.

They were standing five feet apart. Jack took a step closer as he spoke.

'I'm not. I'm as Irish as you are.'

Willie backed away.

'Why were you following me?'

'You ran away – I just chased you. Do you not remember me?'

'No.'

'A couple of nights back we met, but we got separated. There were soldiers. I was worried about you.'

Willie was suddenly angry.

'What do you mean, soldiers? The soldiers all talk the same as you. Are you one of them?'

'No, no, Willie. I'm a friend. I didn't mean to upset you.'

'You didn't.' The boy was cross. 'It's just suspicious – you showing up today of all days.'

'Why what's today?'

Willie eyed him for a moment silently.

'Listen, if you're straight with me I'll see you don't get harmed. Who sent you?'

'Nobody sent me, Willie.' Jack could feel tears beginning to burn at the backs of his eyes. 'Don't you remember? You said my shoes looked comfy? Please, I'm not lying.'

'There is something familiar about you alright, but I think I'd remember if I met you.'

'You did, Willie, or else how would I know your name?'

'That house I went into – do you know who lives there?' Willie asked.

'No, how could I?'

'If you were a spy you might know.'

'A spy?'

'Yes, a spy. The Castle has people everywhere. You could be one of them for all I know.'

'I'm a twelve year old boy, Willie, I'm not a spy. Look at me. Do you think I'd be going around dressed like this if I was a spy?'

Willie smiled.

'I'd be the worst spy ever!' Jack said.

'You would, right enough,' Willie laughed.

'I need to find my way back to my Grandfather's house on Haroldville Avenue – can you show me the way?'

'Come on with me so. You're a strange fella Jack, do you know that?'

'I suppose I am.'

Jack followed Willie out onto the street, amazed that he had found this boy again.

'You really don't remember me Willie, do you, from the other night?' he asked.

'No, I don't. Are you sure it was me?'

'Of course. This is Dublin, isn't it?' Jack asked.

'What sort of question is that man? Where else would it be, Timbuktu?'

'Okay, but what day is it?'

'Have you had a bang on the head Jack? Is that it? It's Monday of course. Bank holiday Monday.'

'But what date?'

'The 24th of April!'

'Yes, yes, but what year?'

'What year? 1916 of course!'

'The 24th of April 1916! It's the Rising, that's it!' Jack shouted.

Willie turned to him and grabbed him roughly by the collar of his t-shirt.

'Keep your voice down! What do you know about it anyway?' Willie pushed him against the railings of a house. Some men passing by glared at them, but none of them said anything.

'My Grandad,' Jack mumbled. 'My Grandad told me about it.'

'Is he a volunteer? What's his name?'

'Michael O'Connor,' Jack said. 'He's too old to fight, but I think he would have liked to.'

'Well he shouldn't be blabbing – that kind of thing can get a fella shot!'

Willie released his grip and they walked on in silence for a while longer. Another packed tram passed them by, this one with the word *Bovril* in large letters on the front.

'Where is everyone going anyway?' Jack asked.

'It's a holiday. They're going out to Sandymount to the seaside or the races most likely, those that has money at any rate.'

'And you? What are you doing?'

'I'm working.'

'You have to work Willie?'

'I'm a paper boy, but today I'm working for the cause Jack, for Ireland.'

'Is that what you were doing just now? That wasn't a newspaper you were delivering, was it?'

Willie stopped again and looked at him.

'You ask an awful lot of questions, you know that?'

'Sorry, I'm just interested that's all. Will you be fighting?'

Willie pushed out his chest and threw his shoulders back.

'I might be,' he said. 'I'm awaiting orders. I'm going to report to Commandant de Valera at four o'clock at Boland's Mill.'

Jack remembered that name from his visit to the museum, and now he wished he had listened more attentively when Grandad was reading the displays. This year was the centenary of the Rising and the museum had many new exhibits in place to mark the occasion. Jack was very bright at school and usually soaked up facts, but he had been in a sulk that day and now he found it impossible to recall the names of others involved in the fighting. In fact he had no idea how extensive the fighting had been in the city, but he had the impression that it had not been that bad. They had walked past the GPO when they were on O'Connell Street and Grandad had shown him a bronze statue of the dying Cú Chulainn with a crow perched on his shoulder. He told him that this was the place where the Proclamation of the Republic was read, but Jack just wondered what that had to do with some giant from an ancient folk tale.

'Can I go with you?' he asked Willie.

'Go where with me?'

'To the Rising – to the GPO.'

Willie stopped in his tracks again.

'How do you know so much?'

Jack frantically tried to think of something plausible.

'I don't know anything!'

Willie looked at him.

'It's my Grandad – he seems to know an awful lot about the Rising, but I promise you he hasn't told anyone, apart from me that is.'

'He must be in the know. Is he friends with Pearse or Clarke?'

'I think he is. He certainly admires those men.'

They started walking again, Jack following Willie.

'So can I go with you?'

'We'll see.'

'That's what mothers say when they mean no.'

Willie smiled at him.

'You're right Jack – that's very clever.'

'So can I?'

'Later on. I'll call for you. Here's your street now.'

Jack looked up and recognised his Grandad's street, once more devoid of traffic. He wondered what he'd do when he reached the house.

Willie stood out on the pavement while Jack approached the door.

'I don't have a key,' he said over his shoulder. 'I'll have to knock.'

He raised his hand slowly and lifted the knocker and let it fall twice. There was silence within for a moment and then he heard footsteps. He placed his hand on his heart and felt his pulse quicken. The door opened and Grandad was standing before him.

'Jack! What are doing outside, I thought you were still in bed.'

'I… I… don't know.'

The shadow of a memory spread across his sleeping consciousness and he looked round. The street was empty but for lines of parked cars, the morning sunlight glinting off their windscreens. Grandad took him gently by the arm and led him inside.

Chapter 6

Jack felt better after he ate breakfast and drank a mug of Grandad's strong, sweet tea.

'Do you sleepwalk often then?' Grandad asked.

'No, never.'

'There's obviously something worrying you son.'

'No. No, Grandad I'm fine. I'm just tired really, like I haven't slept at all.'

They sat opposite each other sipping their tea in silence for a moment.

'Could we go to the museum again today, Grandad? I'd like to learn more about the Rising.'

Grandad smiled broadly.

'Of course we can Jack, straight after we fix Mrs. Morrison's radiators.' He winked at Jack, stood up and threw the last of his tea down the sink.

Later that morning Mrs. Morrison made more tea for Grandad while he tramped around the house checking radiators and the water tank in the attic and Peadar and Jack played football out on the street. They lived on a street parallel to Grandad's, but it looked very much the same to Jack. All the time Jack was looking out for Sally, half in fear and half in awe of her. But she didn't seem to be home and he was too embarrassed to ask Peadar where she was. Eventually she descended from her room and came out onto the street where the boys were playing. She walked up to

Jack who, from the moment he saw her, had lost all interest in the game.

'Do you want to go to the canal?' she asked him.

Jack nodded. He'd seen the canal before and it was a dank and depressing sight, full of rubbish of all sorts, shopping trolleys, bicycles, burst footballs, car tyres and plastic bags.

'What about our game Jack?' Peadar shouted from across the road.

Jack simply shrugged his shoulders as if that was somehow an adequate explanation for his quitting the game so soon. Peadar didn't protest.

'I'm coming too,' he said simply.

The three of them walked in silence for a while and Jack realised that he was not enjoying himself. He had imagined that being in Sally's company would make him feel better, that simply by looking at her he would feel some sort of happiness, but it wasn't the case at all. He felt knotted and worried inside, overly conscious of his actions and his words, hearing his own voice and his accent when he spoke as if it was a bad reflection on him somehow.

'You don't say much, do you?' Sally looked at him.

'I suppose not.'

'I suppose not!' Sally mimicked him now and he reddened again. How unfair it was that he had no control over his own body, that he could betray himself and show his embarrassment so easily.

'Leave him alone Sally!' Peadar's reprimand was more a plea than a command.

Jack could see that Peadar was used to giving in to his older sister.

Nothing was said for a while until they reached the canal.

'God it's a mess isn't it?' Sally laughed. She looked at him, her brown eyes open wide, expecting an answer.

'It's okay,' he said. 'Grandad brought me here the other day and I thought it was nice.'

Sally looked at him.

'This is *nice*?' she asked, pointing at an overflowing bin beside the water.

'Oh I don't know,' Peadar said. 'Some days when the swans are here and the sun is reflected on the water it can be beautiful.'

Sally ignored her brother.

'So what's the story Jack, why are you visiting Dublin?' she asked.

'I don't really know to be honest. My mum has some stuff she needs to sort out I think, so I'm just staying here for a little while.'

'Stuff?' Sally looked perplexed. 'You mean *man trouble*!'

'Just stuff,' Jack said.

Jack could see that Peadar was becoming agitated, his eyes moving from him to Sally and back as if he was a spectator at a tennis match.

'My mam says that your mam and your step-dad are splitting up – is that it?'

'Sally, for God's sake, you can't ask him that!' Peadar was horrified.

Jack turned away and started walking along the canal bank.

Peadar hurried after him. 'I'm sorry Jack, she doesn't mean to be so cruel – I promise. She doesn't know what being subtle is, you know?' He smiled at Jack.

Jack nodded and smiled back and they walked along the canal a little together. Sally didn't follow them. Jack looked back and saw that she was talking to a group of teenagers who had just arrived.

'It must be cool living in London though. What's it like?' Peadar asked.

'I suppose it's just like living here. You go to school every day, you play football, you go to a friend's house, you hang out.'

'Ah I'd say it's brilliant! Better than this kip anyway. When I grow up I'm going to live in London – or Paris maybe, or New York. I'll be as posh as you are.'

'I'm not posh.'

'Well, I mean rich.'

'I'm not that either.'

'Are you not?'

'No, we live in a small house, and I go to an ordinary school like everybody else – nothing special.'

'But you sound posh.' Peadar seemed disappointed.

'No, not posh, just different because I'm not from here.'

They walked along a little bit more. There were swans among the rushes as they approached the lock. Up close they were beautiful, sleek and powerful looking. Jack felt sorry for them, living in such a drab place. He thought about how different people's lives could be and at the same time how similar they were in many ways too. He was thinking of Peadar. He was thinking of Willie too.

'Did you ever hear the story of the Children of Lir?' Peadar asked.

'No.'

'They were turned into swans by their wicked stepmother.'

'That sounds familiar,' Jack said.

'I know it's ridiculous, but every time I see a swan I think that it's really a child in disguise.'

The boys looked at each other for a moment in silence and then sniggered.

'I know, I know,' Peadar laughed, 'it's a bit mad isn't it?'

Jack nodded and they both laughed as they walked on.

'Do you like it here Jack?' Peadar asked.

'I'm beginning to.' He smiled at him. Peadar smiled back.

The knot inside his guts had begun to unravel. He felt calm. He would almost have said happy.

They sat down on a bench beside the lock and watched the swans come and go. They talked about football and music and school, the subjects they enjoyed and the teachers who annoyed them most. Jack forgot about London for a while and he forgot about his mum too.

On the far side of the canal a cyclist stopped and was looking across at them, shielding his eyes with his hands from the afternoon sun.

'Oh God!' Peadar said.

'What is it?' Jack asked.

'Nothing, nothing. Don't look across at him, but that bloke on the bike, he's bad news.'

Jack looked across and saw Biker staring back at him.

'I told you not to look Jack! For God's sake!'

'I know him,' Jack said matter-of-factly, 'I met him the other day.'

'You what?'

'He'd tried to rob me, him and another, older, ugly boy, but Grandad chased them away.'

'Do you think he recognises you?'

'I don't know. I don't care to be honest,' Jack said.

'His name is Paddy Barton and the older fella he hangs around with is Trevor Kelly. Kelly's a dangerous fella. Stay well clear of them Jack, promise me.'

Peadar looked at him.

'I promise,' Jack said.

Still he couldn't keep his eyes off the figure on the bicycle across the canal. Biker raised a hand and waved at them before pedalling off in the direction of Dolphin's Barn.

On their way back home Jack began to tell Peadar about his first meeting with Willie. Sally was waiting for them where they had left her, but she was alone now. Jack did not feel like talking anymore when he saw her. Depending on Peadar's reaction he might tell him about the second time they met. Just as they turned the corner onto their street he saw the long-haired man he had seen days before outside his Grandad's house. He was waiting on the footpath up ahead and they would have to pass by him.

'Do you know him?' Jack asked.

'No,' Peadar said.

'That gawky-looking fella with the hair? I do not!' Sally said.

'I saw him a couple of days ago outside our house; I think he wants to talk to me.'

'Don't talk to him Jack, just ignore him. You can't trust anyone these days!' Peadar said.

As they approached him, the man smiled at them. Jack thought he looked a little crazy, so he studied the ground below him as he walked past.

'Are you an O'Connor?' the man asked.

Jack felt sick suddenly. He stopped, unable to make himself walk on again. The worst had happened. The stranger had spoken to him; he even knew who he was. He tried to land on a plausible reason for this man's appearance, but was unable to come up with anything amid the headlong rush of fear and anxiety he felt.

'Ye-yes,' he stammered.

'You get out of here!' Sally shouted at the man.

The man cowered at the sound of her raised voice. Jack saw that he was frightened too.

'You heard me, get on out of here before I get the cops! I can scream a whole lot louder than this!'

The stranger hesitated before turning on his heel and hurrying down the road.

'Are you alright Jack?' Peadar asked.

Sally turned to him and made to put her arms around him. He recoiled. There was no one he wanted right now, no one but his mother. He wished they all would just leave him alone. He walked on and Sally and Peadar followed a little way behind.

When they got inside Grandad was sitting at the kitchen table, drinking another mug of tea and chatting to Mrs. Morrison.

Peadar burst in the door ahead of them.

'Mam, Mam – some fella tried to talk to Jack on the way home, but Sally ran him!'

Jack's face felt hot, his head felt light. Grandad had finished his work and had left the heat on as a test. The repaired radiators gave off a cloying heat.

That afternoon he and Grandad walked into town and along by the river towards the museum. As they walked Jack noted the names of the streets that they passed, some of which were familiar to him from his time spent with Willie.

When they got to the museum it was crowded and Jack led the way to the new exhibits. A film about the Rising was being shown, grainy black and white footage taken at that time. Jack recognised the trams and the horse drawn carts and the peculiar formal clothes that the men and women wore. Then there were pictures of children playing in the street. They were dirty and bare-footed mainly, but smiling shyly for the camera. He thought he might see Willie among them.

The footage jumped and changed now. Buildings reduced to rubble with smoke or dust rising; a naval gun boat on the Liffey; people standing around or poking among the ruins of shops or houses. Tired looking men were marched out of dark buildings with their arms raised, giving themselves up to soldiers with bayoneted guns aimed at their chests. Every movement was hurried and jerky, as if there was no time to be lost.

Gangs of grey men were ushered along streets between lines of armed soldiers. Some of the men had bandages on their heads, their arms in slings. Rows of injured rebels lay on stretchers in the road, perhaps some of them were already dead.

Jack leaned in towards Grandad.

'Did any children die in the Rising?' he asked.

'They did I believe. There's something about it further on in the museum.'

Jack's mouth went dry and he could feel his heart beat in his chest.

'Will they have all the names of the kids, Grandad?'

'I think so – there was someone on the radio last week talking about it.'

They walked on through the exhibits, stopping here and there to look at the photographs and read from the panels. Jack saw a picture of Eamon Ceannt, commander at the South Dublin Union, a sad looking man with dark eyes and a large waxed moustache. Grandad explained how the Union was now the site of St. James's hospital. They could walk up to it on their way home, he said.

When they came to the section called *Children of the Rising* Jack wanted to leave. He was afraid that he would see a picture of Willie or that his name might appear on a list of casualties. He was only a child. Even though he said he might fight, surely he would never have been allowed to take part.

'Come here Jack, this is what you were asking about.' Grandad was standing in front of a bronze plaque with a long list of names on it.

'It says here that forty children died in the Rising. Their names are all here.'

Jack turned quickly and walked in the opposite direction. He stopped by a huge photo of O'Connell Street in ruins – or Sackville Street as it was then. He studied the picture closely, breathing deeply, waiting for the shake in his hands to ease off.

Grandad came and stood beside him after a while.

'Are you okay Jack?'

'Yeah, I'm fine. It's just so sad those kids getting killed.'

'It is, yes of course. They were blameless in all of it. Shot in the cross-fire in most cases it seems.'

'Kids my own age?' Jack asked.

'Yes, and some even younger I think. But at least they're acknowledged now. I never thought about the children involved before now. It's hard to believe, isn't it?'

'Can we go now Grandad?'

'Yes, of course.'

Jack was happy to be outside again. He needed the air. On the way home the old man related all of the new information he'd gathered that day: two hundred and sixty two civilians killed, two thousand two hundred and seventeen civilians wounded.

'That's a lot of people whatever way you look at it. Most of them killed by the British, mind you.'

Jack did not reply; it seemed that there was no reply expected.

Grandad stopped suddenly on the street, turned to Jack and closed his eyes.

'The Republic guarantees religious and civil liberty, equal rights and equal opportunities to all its citizens, and declares its resolve to pursue the happiness and prosperity of the whole nation and of all its parts, cherishing all the children of the nation equally...'

He stopped.

'That's part of the Proclamation,' he said. 'I learned it off years ago.' He shook his head sadly.

Jack looked up at him. He had that peculiar look in his eyes again, as if he might be angry.

'It didn't work out quite the way they hoped and that's for sure,' was all he said.

Jack wasn't sure what he meant, but he sensed that he was more dejected than cross and thought it best to say nothing. As they crossed the busy street he took his Grandad's hand and was happy to feel the warmth of the old man's hand on his.

Chapter 7

It was good to have people around, even if they were all old men. Jack enjoyed the funny things they said to each other, or *slagging* as Grandad called it, even when some of it was directed at him. His London accent was always a talking point, but so was Sally Morrison whose name had been mentioned more than once by Grandad in the days after her visit with her brother. He was annoyed at first but he'd grown fond of Grandad and found it hard to stay mad at him for very long. For a while Jack forgot his own worries about his mother and his uncertain future as he helped Grandad get the room ready for the card game. The men were all like Grandad; they were old and they were Dublin born and bred and they looked a little scary when he met them first but, reassured by Grandad's presence, Jack soon overcame his fear of them and allowed himself to take part in the conversation before the poker game started.

'Is this a new bar man you have here Mick? He's a bit on the small side,' Doyler said. Doyler was a tall, skinny, bald man of seventy odd years. His hands were covered in dark brown blotches, the fingers permanently clawed and the knuckles enlarged.

'Yeah, he only serves shorts, isn't that right young Jack?' Tommy laughed. Tommy looked younger, a squat man with a smiling red face and flowing white hair combed back from a high forehead. He looked like a man who laughed a lot.

'Is that his name – Jack? Is it Jack O'Connor?' Johnner, a dark-eyed, serious looking old man with a lined face and short cropped silver hair, shook his head at Grandad. 'I swear to God Mick, I can't believe yous named him after a Kerry football manager!'

'Leave the lad alone now, will ya? He's helping me get things sorted out here, but he'll be going up to bed now shortly.'

'Do you know anything about football young Jack?' Tommy asked.

'I love football!'

'Ah, who doesn't – who do you support then?' Tommy asked.

'Arsenal, they're the best team by miles.'

'Are ya joking, United are the only team, even since Ferguson retired.' Doyler, smiling, pulled up his shirt sleeve and showed Jack a red and black devil tattoo on his upper arm with the letters MUFC underneath.

'Will ya put that thing away for God's sake! That's not real football at all.' Johnner looked at Jack fiercely. 'Did you ever see a Gaelic Football match?' He demanded.

'Eh... no.'

'Come on now Mick you have to put that right. Dublin are playing Cork in the league on Sunday, you should bring him along to it.' Johnner poked Grandad on the shoulder with his extended finger.

'Leave me alone, will you? I haven't been to a match in years,' Grandad said.

'I'd love to go Grandad if we could!' Jack said.

'You see, the lad is interested, you have to bring him now, doesn't he lads?' Johnner looked like he was smiling. It didn't really suit him, Jack thought.

'Looks like you'll have to bring him so,' Tommy said.

'Sure maybe we'll all go, I haven't seen the Dubs in ages either!' Doyler was rubbing his hands together.

'You feck off back to Old Trafford you West Brit!' Jack guessed Johnner was joking but he couldn't be completely sure.

'Can we go to the match Grandad, please?' he asked.

'We'll see,' Grandad said.

'That's what adults always say when they mean no, Grandad!' Jack said.

All the old men laughed loudly at that.

'Ah, he has your card marked well and truly there Mick!' Doyler rubbed his hands together and tilted his head to one side.

The laughter died off. Jack could see that the men were itching to start the game. Grandad had gone to the fridge and returned with three cans of beer and lemonades for himself and Jack.

'I hear Mick's been teaching you about the Rising young Jack? Is that right?' Tommy asked.

The centenary of the Rising was imminent. Wherever you went people were talking about it and it was in all the newspapers, and on the television and radio experts and historians discussed the legacy of the Rising and argued at length with each other, sometimes angrily, over what it meant to be an Irish person living now.

'Yes. Grandad knows an awful lot about it.' Jack happily drank his cold drink, the bubbles fizzing against his nose, making him want to sneeze.

'Well, he thinks he does,' quipped Doyler.

'I bloomin' well do!' Grandad said with a smirk.

Johnner took a long drink of his glass of stout and pulled a face as if it tasted foul. Jack wondered why he drank the stuff at all.

'I know more than you lot anyways,' Grandad said.

'Now, now, lads. Don't be arguing.' Tommy said, laughing.

'We went to the museum,' Jack said, wanting to let them know that his grandad knew what he was talking about, 'and Grandad knows the Proclamation off by heart.'

'There's one thing knowing what's in it and another thing living it,' Johnner said darkly.

'Ah come off it now Johnner and don't be so serious,' Doyler put in. 'We're only here to have a friendly game of cards, not to have a political discussion.' He rubbed his hands together and tilted his head to the side again.

'I'm only sayin,' Johnner said.

'Come on you,' Grandad said to Jack, getting to his feet. 'You don't want to be listening to a bunch of old cranks. It's time for bed anyway.'

Jack didn't want to go up. He liked to be among Grandad's friends. They all seemed nice, even Johnner in his own peculiar way.

After he brushed his teeth, Jack stood out on the landing trying to pick up bits of the conversation from below. They seemed to be arguing about something and Jack tentatively took a step down the stairs in order to hear more clearly. On the third step the old boards let out a high pitched squeal and he froze. The conversation seemed to stop just at the same time and Jack stood where he was, frantically trying to think of an excuse when the door would inevitably open and Grandad's cross face would appear. A glass of water! That was it! He had a sore throat and needed a glass of water.

But the door did not open and the conversation resumed after a moment as if it had never broken at all. He crept back up the stairs and closed his room door quietly behind him.

He got into bed and pulled his grandmother's blanket around him, for comfort as much as for warmth, and he shut his eyes tight. But sleep didn't come for a long time. *Huntington's Disease.* The words were lodged in his head now. He thought about how his grandmother must have suffered. It must have been really bad for Grandad to be glad when she passed on. Then he thought about his mother for a while. It seemed like ages since he'd seen her, but in fact it had only been a couple of days. He shivered and pulled his grandmother's blanket around him, wondering why he did not have the courage to look at the list of names at the museum. He listened to the muffled voices from below until the last voice had been put out and the front door closed behind it. He listened to his grandad moving about downstairs alone and he was still awake to hear his solitary footsteps tramp up the stairs to bed.

When Grandad put his head around the door to check on him moments later, Jack kept his eyes shut and tried to breathe evenly until he closed the door again. It was only after Grandad shut his own room door that Jack finally relaxed and let sleep in.

Chapter 8

The soldiers were marching down a tree lined road. Jack walked along beside them on the pavement among a crowd of cheering people, some of whom clapped and shouted *God Save The King!*

They looked old and worn out from what had obviously been a long march in the warm sunshine: their uniforms shabby, their rifles ancient; but to his eye they marched with an impressive precision all the same.

Willie appeared by his side and caught his sleeve.

'I'd stay back here a bit out of the way if I were you Jack,' he said.

'Oh Willie there you are. It looks like trouble for the volunteers. There must be hundreds of them,' Jack said.

'Don't worry about those lads! They're just on their way to the barracks. Every soldier in the city must be on leave today if the Gorgeous Wrecks have been called up.'

'Gorgeous Wrecks?' Jack asked.

'Yeah,' Willie laughed, 'that's what we call them; they're not real soldiers – see there, on their tunics, it says *Georgius Rex*.'

'But they're armed and ready for battle,' Jack said.

'These fellas won't be doing any fighting Jack. Look at them! They're all oul' fellas, they're not even proper soldiers.'

The soldiers were just approaching a bridge over the canal on their way into town when a lone shot rang out. Jack saw the officer who was leading the group fall to his knees. Blood was flowing freely from his head. Suddenly there was mayhem as soldiers and onlookers ran for cover. Willie pulled Jack by the sleeve into the front garden of a nearby house where they hid behind a flowering cherry tree.

More shots were fired and here and there soldiers fell, some writhing in pain, while others slumped motionless as if they were dead. Jack thought of the Playstation games that he played with his friends before his mother came home from work; the over 18's war games they weren't supposed to play.

'This is really happening!' Jack said the words out loud.

'It bloomin' well is Jack!' Willie confirmed.

The soldiers had found cover wherever they could, behind trees and hedges or hunched below the stone steps at the entrances of houses. One very old man lay flat on his stomach inside a low garden wall, his useless gun discarded as he ran.

'Why aren't they firing back, Willie?'

'They can't see where the snipers are.'

Jack was impressed by Willie's knowledge of urban warfare.

'They must be in one of those houses on the far side of the bridge.' Willie pointed at a tall building with large double windows on each floor on the corner of Mount Street Lower and Clanwilliam Place.

Jack looked at the windows of the house but could see nothing move. There was silence for a while and the soldiers reluctantly emerged from their hiding places and formed a less formal troop in the middle of the road. To his horror they began their march again towards the bridge and again the snipers opened fire. More soldiers fell, while the others quickly withdrew.

'Why did they do that?' Jack was appalled. The smell of the gunpowder and the sight of the blood on the road made his head spin.

'They're soldiers; that's what they do,' Willie said.

'But they didn't even fire back at them?'

'I know. Come on.'

Willie led Jack away some distance from the bridge and sat him down on the kerb.

'It's hard the first time, I know,' he said.

'What do you mean? What's hard?' Jack asked.

'When you see someone get shot the first time, it's hard.'

'You've seen this before?'

'Yes. My brother Seán was shot in the riots during the Lockout. I'll never forget when they brought him home. There was blood everywhere.'

'And did he... is he?'

'Oh he lived alright. He's with Connolly now in the GPO.'

'Is he not afraid he'll get shot again?' Jack asked.

'He doesn't care – he's fighting for Ireland, that's all that matters.'

They stayed where they were for some time, hearing occasional gun shots, and eventually an ambulance arrived to take the wounded to hospital.

'We ought to take a message back to Boland's Mill, to Commandant de Valera, to let him know what's happening on the bridge,' Willie said.

Jack was bothered by the way de Valera's men had shot the Gorgeous Wrecks. A bunch of old men playing at war games had been shot without returning fire or without being given a chance to escape. It didn't seem to bother Willie much, but then he had seen his own brother get shot in the past. Jack wondered how anyone could get used to this kind of violence. For the first time he began to wonder about the men who had started the Rising. Grandad called them Freedom Fighters, but now Jack had seen their fighting first hand he was less sure about their cause.

'Come with me now,' Willie said and he turned and jogged off down the street. Jack followed him reluctantly, but he did not know what else he could do. Willie studied each house as he ran past and stopped only when he came to one where a large black bicycle leaned against a wall under the front window. He opened the gate and silently led the bike out onto the road.

'What are you doing?' Jack asked.

'I'm commandeering this bicycle on behalf of the Provisional Government of the Irish Republic,' Willie said. 'Now hop on the back there till we carry out our mission!'

Jack threw his leg over the back wheel and sat on the carrier. It was hard and painful to sit on. Willie was too small to throw his leg over the bicycle so he bent his body under the cross bar and somehow pressed down hard on the pedal and pushed the bike off. Jack kept his legs out so that he avoided the grinding of the rusted chain, and Willie, his small body bent around the high frame of the old bike, managed to stand on the pedals and at the same time steer the thing down the empty street.

They headed back down Northumberland Road and took a left onto a wide tree-lined street that was dominated by a huge church. When they came to the next junction they veered left under a railway bridge and kept on going until they reached Ringsend Road where they bore left until they came to Grand

Canal Dock. At Boland's Mill all seemed quiet. There were no signs of any soldiers in the immediate vicinity. Or rebels for that matter.

Willie stopped pedalling and Jack climbed off the carrier. Willie left the bike against a wall and they walked around the Dock looking up at the tall windows of the mill, but they could see no sign of life.

'Hey, you there, what do you want?' A voice whispered urgently from behind a heavy wooden door.

'We're here to see the Commandant,' Willie said importantly, 'we have news from Mount Street Bridge.'

The door opened slowly, but it was dark inside and they could not see who was there. Willie whispered to Jack as they entered.

'You better let me do the talking. That accent of yours could cause problems.'

Inside their eyes adjusted to the darkness enough so that they could see a man before them and in the background others sitting around idly. The place was a mess. Chairs and tables had been piled up against the windows, most of which had been broken from the inside.

'You want to see himself then?' The man who had opened the door smiled at them.

He did not look like much of a soldier, Jack thought. None of the volunteers did. They had no uniforms to speak of and the guns and rifles they carried were all different, some looked worn and rusted like they might explode in the hands of whoever might be foolish enough to fire them.

They followed the man up two flights of stairs until they came to rooms that obviously were offices in the factory. The man knocked on the door of the first of these and a voice was heard to say: 'Enter'.

A very tall figure stood with his back to them looking out over the dock.

'Commandant, these two lads were down at the Bridge just now and are bringing news.'

Commandant de Valera turned around to inspect them. He was a tall, imposing man with thick dark hair and a full moustache. He looked like a soldier, immaculately turned out in dark green uniform and knee length brown leather boots. Jack wanted to hate him but in fact he was more fascinated than angry. His face was stern, as if shaped from ice or stone and two dark eyes studied Jack and Willie for a moment before he spoke.

'Well, my fine young lads, what news have you brought for me?'

'Sir, the soldiers have been turned back at the bridge. The Volunteers picked off those at the front and the rest were scattered.' Jack was impressed by the way Willie gave the news, but he was even more impressed by de Valera's reaction.

'You've done well boys. You should be proud that you have served your country in her time of need, but now I want you to go home.'

'But sir, we can do more. If you have messages to be delivered to comrades around the city we can do it for you, Jack and me – I have a bicycle.'

'Does your friend not talk at all?' de Valera said.

'I can talk alright,' Jack said. His voice sounded strange, not like his own. It sounded English, but then he remembered that that was how he spoke. After all he was English really, he was born in England; he'd never even been to Ireland before this last week.

De Valera smiled. Jack thought his heart would burst, it beat so fast.

'So we have a Sassenach among us, do we?'

'I suppose,' Jack said, feeling braver now that he had actually said something to this terrifying-looking man.

De Valera reached out and put his hand on Jack's shoulder. Jack could still feel its weight long after he'd removed it.

'The people of Ireland applaud your sense of justice, a mhic. It's good that you are helping, but...'

'We want to help sir!' Willie couldn't stop himself.

De Valera raised his hand and Willie fell silent.

'I want you to go home now, back to your mothers and fathers where you will be safe.'

Jack thought of his mother again wherever she was, and he bit his lower lip hard to keep the tears at bay.

'You have done well, both of you, but you are too young. The day will come in time when you will be called upon to serve your country and I am heartened by your eagerness. But wait for that day... What are your names?'

'Willie sir, and this is Jack.'

'Well, Willie, Jack. I salute you and wish you well!' And with that he brought his right hand up to his brow and saluted. Then he returned to his place at the window and his contemplation of the world below him. He was very impressive, Jack decided. It was no surprise that men were prepared to follow him, to die for him, and to kill for him too.

Jack knew there was no point in trying to say anything more, and even Willie seemed to accept it too. Jack would have liked to tell him how the Gorgeous Wrecks would not return fire, but the moment had passed. They followed the man back down the stairs before he let them out into the yard again. The bike was where they had left it and, as Willie struggled to get it standing again, Jack wondered where they would go from here. They mounted awkwardly and this time Willie continued on the way they had come, along Ringsend Road until they came to Great Brunswick Street. The city was silent, as if waiting for something to happen, the way his street in London was on those mornings when he woke very early, before the first bus arrived, before the noise of the street sweeping machine announced day had begun. But it was late afternoon now and there was no one around as they cycled towards the city centre. It was not at all like there was a war on.

'Where are we going now?' Jack shouted ahead to Willie, who was pedalling as fast as he could go.

'To the GPO,' he called over his shoulder. 'Seán is there, with Connolly and Pearse. They might have need of us yet!'

Just as he said those words a dog ran out under the wheels of the bicycle and sent them flying to the ground. When Jack opened his eyes he was lying in the road and all he could see was a bicycle lying on its side, its front wheel spinning fast.

Chapter 9

Jack watched the wheel spin. He was reminded of the wheel of fortune at the school fete the year before. He'd spent all his money on tickets but he didn't win anything. He never had any luck.

He could hear a voice, but he wasn't sure what it was saying. Then he remembered Willie and the dog running out in front of them.

'Are you okay Willie?' he asked.

'Who's Willie?'

Jack didn't recognise the voice. He tried to turn his head away from the wheel but he couldn't seem to do it.

'Are you okay Jack? It's Jack, isn't it?'

Jack felt unwell, sick in his stomach, but worried also. How did this person know his name?

He felt two hands grip him under his arms.

'Try to stand and see how you are.' The voice was close beside him, a peculiar Irish accent, not like Grandad's, but full of concern.

'Leave me alone!' Jack wrenched himself free of the man, but found it hard to stand on his own. His head felt light.

'Come on, let me help you back to your grandad's house, it's not that far.'

Jack tried to focus on where the voice was coming from. It was the young man he had seen before, the one who had tried to talk to him when he was with Peadar and Sally. What did he want with him?

'I'm okay, I'm okay,' Jack protested, but as he tried to walk his knees gave way and the man just about managed to grab him before he fell.

'It's okay, I have you,' he said. 'Can you walk?'

Overcome by fatigue Jack let his anxiety fall away. He felt so weak and tired. He walked or was half-carried along.

'I can come back for your bicycle,' he said.

'I don't have a bicycle,' Jack said absently.

'But I saw you fall off it just now. Who owns it then?'

'I don't know,' Jack said. And he didn't know.

'You mentioned someone called Willie when I came over to you first. Is Willie your brother?'

'No. He's my friend. I don't have a brother.'

'So where did you get the bike?' the man asked.

Jack was confused and tired of all the questions. It was hard to know what was real anymore. He thought he might wake at any moment and be lying in bed in that musty old room in Grandad's house. Or maybe he might wake up and be with Willie back in 1916. Everything had become so unfamiliar since he came here anyway that it didn't seem to matter where he was anymore.

He looked up at the man as they walked. He was tall and had a kind face Jack thought.

'I commandeered it on behalf of the Provisional Government of the Irish Republic,' Jack said to himself.

'You what?'

'Nothing.'

They walked on for a while in silence, and as they did Jack became more aware of his surroundings. He was getting near home. He tried to remember exactly what had happened.

'How do you know my name?' He asked.

The man was silent for a few moments. He hesitated before he finally spoke.

'I don't,' he said.

Jack knew he was lying.

'You called me Jack when you came over first.'

'Did I?'

'You did.'

'I must have heard your friend say it the other day.'

'What friend?'

'That girl, the rude girl you were with.'

'Sally?'

'Yeah, her. She must have called you Jack then. I'm Robert, by the way.'

They fell silent again.

'You don't mind me asking, do you,' Robert began, 'but why are you wearing pyjamas?'

'I'm not.'

'Well, you are I'm afraid, pyjama bottoms and a t-shirt.'

'I sleep walk,' Jack said, defensively. He had to think of something.

'This far?' Robert was incredulous. 'But I saw you riding that bike!'

There were too many things going on in his life now that Jack could not explain. This last was just a tiny thing, almost nothing compared to the time he'd been spending in the past in Willie's company.

They were at Grandad's at last. Jack didn't say anything more as they walked on, and Robert fell silent when he realised Jack was not going to explain how he came to be cycling and sleeping at the same time. Robert pushed the bell and they waited for the door to open. Jack thought he heard Robert muttering under his breath, as if he was nervously reciting a speech he was about to deliver.

Grandad looked fierce when he saw Jack. He ignored Robert.

'I've been worried sick about you all morning, Jack. I was just on the point of calling the Guards.'

'I found him on the South Circular Road, he'd come off his bike,' Robert said.

Grandad looked at him as if he was mad.

'What?'

'He had a tumble from his bike, that's all. No harm done I think, nothing broken anyway. Just got a bit of a shake.'

Grandad shook his head and looked long and hard at Robert. All three were still standing at the door.

'He doesn't have a bike!' Grandad said.

'Well he was riding somebody's bike just now and he fell off.' Robert was becoming impatient.

'Sorry. I'm sorry. Who did you say you were?' Grandad asked.

'I didn't,' Robert said. 'My name is Robert. Robert Burke.'

'Well, thank you for bringing him home,' Grandad said, but Jack could tell that Grandad was not grateful at all or pleased for that matter. He looked cross. Jack knew he would be in trouble for going out on his own again without saying anything to Grandad, but it was the old man's fault really. After all, he was the adult and he was not looking after Jack properly. If Mum knew what was going on she would not be happy about it.

'You're welcome,' Robert said, but there was a catch in his voice that told Jack that the opposite was true. It was as if the two men knew and disliked each other from a previous encounter, but were pretending to be strangers.

Grandad reached out and took Jack by the shoulder.

'Come on in out of that,' he said.

But Robert did not turn to leave. He just stood there. Jack felt again as if he was living in one of his dreams, as if reality was skewed, and something very bad was about to happen.

'Thanks again for your help,' Grandad said in an effort to end the scene at the door, but Robert just nodded and continued to stand there looking at Grandad.

'What? What is it? Is there something more that you want?'

Robert said nothing; he seemed incapable of speech suddenly.

'Do I know you?' The irritation in Grandad's voice was clearly evident. It made Jack close his eyes; he wished he was anywhere but there.

'I want to have a word with you Mr. O'Connor,' Robert said slowly. 'In private please.'

A shadow seemed to cross Grandad's face, as if a large bird had flown above them, and Jack looked up expecting to see a seagull, but there were no birds around. There was a new and peculiar look in Grandad's eyes. It could have been fear.

'How do you know me?' he said. The words came out broken, a barely audible whisper.

'I can explain,' Robert said. 'I just need a few moments of your time – in private if you don't mind.'

Grandad placed his hand on Jack's head then and it appeared he had forgotten to be cross with Jack because when he spoke to him there was a gentleness in his voice.

'Go on upstairs Jack and get washed and dressed like a good lad. I'll call you in a while and we'll have a cup of tea and some toast. Okay?'

He smoothed Jack's tossed hair and nudged him towards the stairs. Jack climbed the stairs slowly, straining to hear what they were going to say as he went, but they did not speak. They waited until they heard Jack's bedroom door slam shut before they spoke again, but Jack had shut the door without going through it first and now he lay on the landing with his head pressed to the banisters, ears cocked.

'Who are you and what do you want?' Grandad hissed.

'Listen I didn't want to do this, but I feel I have no choice. Your daughter led me to believe that we could meet, but now she's broken off all communication so I thought I'd come looking for you instead.'

'What are you on about man? You're raving!' Jack had never heard Grandad so worked up before.

'Let me finish, will you please!' Robert was cross now too and his country accent became more obvious.

'I think maybe you should just leave now.'

'I'm not going anywhere, do you hear me? I've waited too long for this. Your daughter is Kate O'Connor, right? She gave up a child for adoption twenty three years ago, didn't she?'

Jack's heart was beating so fast in his chest. He held his breath, waiting for Grandad's reply, but it didn't come. He gulped in air and started coughing, which must have startled Grandad into action.

'I... I can't talk now,' he said. 'Your timing's off; you'll have to go now.'

Jack heard the front door close heavily.

Grandad stood motionless in the hall, one foot on the first step of the stairs. Jack crawled slowly towards his bedroom door. He imagined Robert standing outside, waiting for the door to be opened again. He didn't want to think about the things he'd said.

'Are you alright up there Jack?' Grandad was coming up the stairs. By the time he reached his room Jack was sitting on the bed.

'There you are.' Grandad walked into the room and stood at the window peering down into the street.

Jack sensed that Robert was still waiting down there.

Grandad turned around and stood with his back to the window, his shoulders heaving as he breathed, but he did not make eye contact with Jack. After a while he checked outside again. He turned back to Jack. Robert had obviously given up and gone away, but Jack knew he would come back.

'Are you okay Jack?' Grandad said.

'I'm fine Grandad.'

'Listen,' Grandad said, but he seemed unsure what Jack was supposed to listen to. 'Listen,' he said again. 'I'm not sure what's going on or who that fella is or thinks he is. So I don't want you to be worried about it. Okay?'

'Okay.'

'Did you sleepwalk again?'

'I think I must have. I'm not sleeping well and when I do I have lots of dreams.'

'Bad dreams? Nightmares?'

'Not really, but strange. I'm just so tired.'

'It's probably just all the upheaval, you know. You coming here without your mam and that. I suppose that's fairly normal.'

Jack nodded.

'Did he say anything to you?'

'Who?'

'Yer man, Robert. When he was bringing you up the road now, did he say anything?'

'Not really.'

'Anything at all?'

'He knew my name – that was weird I thought.'

'Yes.' Grandad considered this.

'Do you know him Grandad? Is that it?'

'I'm not sure. I might, but don't you bother your head with it at all, okay?'

'Okay.'

But Jack's head was bothered. How come Robert hadn't been mentioned before, by Grandad or by Mum? Dublin was a puzzle. Everything here was a secret, a half-kept secret, something that was better off unsaid. This place was all about history, half-learnt stories, snatches of old songs, old photos, mementos, monuments. Like the kids who died in the Rising – it might take a hundred years but in the end everyone has to get remembered.

Grandad turned to leave.

'Grandad?'

'Yes?'

Jack had the words ready to ask but they wouldn't come out. He wished the old man would tell him everything. It would be better to know the truth no matter how bad it was, about everything; about Robert and about his mum. Grandad looked at him. He was never going to say anything, and he knew it.

'We're still going to the match this afternoon, aren't we?' he asked.

'We sure are son, we sure are. We'll get you some tea and toast and then you can put your head down for an hour or two. You'll need all your strength for watching the Dubs later.'

Chapter 10

They caught a bus into town and walked out to Croke Park in the company of droves of people dressed in blue jerseys, some holding flags, others wearing hats and scarves. It was similar to the walk he and Matt made on Saturdays up Holloway Road towards the Emirates Stadium. But there were some differences too. For starters there were hardly any police around compared to the Arsenal matches and he was amazed to see that groups of Cork fans decked out in bright red walked happily amid the blue crowd as they approached the stadium.

Grandad said that it was only a league game so the crowd wouldn't be that big, but when they took their seats in the Cusack Stand the stadium was filling up quite quickly. Cork versus Dublin was always a good game, Grandad told him, because Cork people were of the opinion that they were better than everyone else – and not just in Ireland, but the world! It stuck in their throats that Dublin was the capital, he said.

'Is this not dangerous Grandad?' Jack asked.

'Is what not dangerous?'

Jack lowered his voice. 'There are Cork fans just behind us.'

Grandad laughed.

'We're civilized in this country Jack. We can go and watch a football match without getting into a fight with the opposition.'

'In the Premiership the fans are always kept separate,' Jack said. 'Matt told me that there used to be loads of fighting at matches years ago.'

'Yeah, there used to be killings alright. That's not to say there's never a fight at a Gaelic match, but it's very rare.'

Jack wasn't completely reassured by Grandad's words. He looked around at all the red among the predominantly blue sea of fans. There was one area to their right, behind one of the goals which was all blue.

'Why are there no Cork fans up there?' he asked.

'That's Hill 16,' Grandad said. 'That's where all the die-hard Dublin fans go to watch the matches. You don't often get opposition supporters in there.'

'Here comes Tommy and Johnner, Grandad.'

Grandad looked happy to see them.

'Ah Jack lad, how are ya?' Tommy said, smiling at him.

Johnner nodded and took his seat beside Tommy. Grandad leaned across Jack to talk to them.

'Doyler not coming then?'

'No, he's watching his beloved United in the pub,' Tommy said.

'I thought you'd be above on the Hill,' Grandad said to Johnner.

'Na, the legs can't take all that standing these days.'

'Here Johnner, tell Jack the story of how Hill 16 got its name,' Tommy said.

Johnner looked at Tommy and then at Grandad. 'You know the story Mick, don't you?' he asked.

Grandad shook his head.

'Well it's a very interesting story. When the stadium was first used, Hill 16 was just that – a hill where people stood to get a good view of a match, but it wasn't called Hill 16 then of course. Over time it became known as Hill 60 after a famous hill in Gallipoli where the Royal Dublin Fusiliers incurred heavy losses during the First World War. Well, so it remained during the 20s and 30s until some senior people in the GAA thought it wasn't right that part of their stadium should be named after a British Army battle site. So, hey presto, they called it Hill 16 in honour of the Rising. Rumours started then that the hill was built from the rubble of O'Connell Street after the Rising, but that's just rameish.'

'What's rameish?' Jack asked.

'Crap – sorry, rubbish,' Johnner said.

'It's a good story though, isn't it?' Tommy said laughing.

'In Ireland we're always more concerned with a good story than the truth,' Grandad said.

'If you had a tune you could sing that!' Johnner chipped in. Jack wished the match would start soon; he wasn't sure what they were talking about anyway.

'I blame de Valera you know,' Johnner went on, 'he was the one who set the tone for our so-called new republic. And look at him! Didn't see any action in Boland's Mill at all in the Rising, did he? Went a bit loopy too, by all accounts.'

Jack wanted to say something to defend de Valera, the imposing man he'd met with Willie, but he was daunted by Johnner. Johnner continued: 'The only one of the leaders not to be executed, ha? American citizen how are ya! Sure hadn't Tom Clarke got citizenship too?'

'Here, the teams are coming out!' Tommy pointed across the pitch, and sure enough two sets of players were running on, greeted by a huge roar from the crowd.

'And don't get me started about the Treaty! Talk about a set up or what.'

'Ah leave it now Johnner,' Grandad said. 'We're here for the football.'

Johnner was silent at last and Jack watched as the Dublin and Cork players warmed up at either end of the ground, running up and down, kicking and catching the ball.

'Why are they handling the ball Grandad? They can't all be the goalkeeper.'

Grandad laughed.

'This is Gaelic Football Jack, they're allowed to catch the ball.'

'So why is it called football then?' Jack asked with a smirk.

'Go on outa that!' The old man laughed.

Grandad explained the rules briefly, but nothing prepared Jack for what he saw when the game finally started.

From the moment the referee threw the ball in between four players in the centre of the pitch the pace of the game was frenetic. Each kick was contested and every attempt by a player to get hold of the ball was met by a strong tackle from his opposite number. Jack kept looking at Grandad, asking why the referee was not blowing his whistle for free after free.

'This isn't like soccer Jack, you're allowed to make physical contact in this game.'

At one stage one of the Dublin players went down holding his head. The Cork player had used an attack Jack knew well from the US wrestling he loved to watch on TV, by holding his arm out in front at head height as the Dublin player passed. Clotheslining they called it. At least the ref gave a free that time.

The first half seemed to be over in no time at all. Cork were winning by three points and Johnner was arguing with a red-shirted man behind him over a penalty that should have been given to Dublin. Grandad smiled at Jack.

'Maybe they *should* separate the supporters,' he said, and he winked at Jack and Tommy.

'So what do you make of it Jack?' Tommy asked.

'It's crazy. But good. It's like rugby, but faster and with more skill. I love it when they run with the ball – what did you call it?'

'Soloing.'

'Yeah, I love it when they solo real fast.'

'Will we win, do you think?' Tommy asked.

'I think we will. We were unlucky not to get that penalty. It's hard to know what's a foul and what's not sometimes.'

'Tell me about it!' Tommy laughed.

'Three points is nothing in a football match,' Grandad said. 'It's all to play for in the second half. Come on we'll get something to eat. I can't listen to those two arguing anymore.' He threw a look back at Johnner.

When they got back to their seats Johnner was missing.

'Gone for a pint probably,' Tommy said.

Dublin started the second half very strongly scoring two goals in the first ten minutes. When Johnner came back he was beaming.

'We have them now lads,' he said making sure to turn around and include his red adversary in the conversation.

The second half seemed much longer than the first and Cork didn't give up. They scored four points in a row and Dublin looked in trouble. When they announced that there would be two additional minutes Dublin were leading by just one point. Cork won a free in the middle of the field and their big number eight kicked it long, all the way into the Dublin goal mouth. The ball fell among three or four players and no one could get their hands on it, but one Cork player managed to strike the ball with his boot, deflecting it off a Dublin defender and into the goal. The stadium was stunned into silence for a moment before the red army erupted in cheers. The final whistle was blown and Jack looked at Grandad. The old man could not hide his disappointment. Tommy was shaking his head and swearing under his breath.

'What were they doing? They just needed to clear it, to the wing, anywhere at all for God's sake!'

They remained seated as all around them red supporters cheered and shouted and hugged each other. There seemed to be much more of them now.

Johnner was saying something to the Cork fan behind him again. Jack could only catch bits of it, but enough to tell him there was trouble brewing.

'Come on,' Grandad said, 'let's make a move.'

'What about himself?' Tommy asked, indicating Johnner with his thumb.

'Ah leave him to it,' Grandad said.

Soon they were on the concourse walking out towards the road, and again Jack was amazed the way the Cork and Dublin fans walked out together without any fuss at all. In fact the crowd was muted; even the Cork fans did not gloat the way soccer fans would after a victory. There was no chanting. Jack heard snatches of conversations as he walked; some groups of Dublin fans discussed the match while others had already moved on and were discussing where to go for something to eat or drink.

The three of them were silent on the way back into town for the most part.

'It was a pity Mick, they had it for the taking,' Tommy said as they walked down Gardiner Street.

'Ah sure, that's the way it goes some days,' was all Grandad replied.

'Do you think we should have left Johnner on his own Mick?'

'He'll be alright Tommy.'

'I hope so, but you know what he's like,' Tommy said.

'Why does he get so cross all the time?' Jack looked up at Grandad.

Grandad kept walking and did not reply.

'He's not all bad Jack,' Tommy said. 'He's had a hard time of it.'

'How do you mean?' Jack asked.

Tommy looked at Grandad, a helpless look in his eyes.

'When he was young he got in a lot of trouble and he was sent to a special school. The boys were treated badly there. It scarred him, you know,' Grandad said.

'Was he in prison Grandad?'

'No, no, nothing like that. He was just a kid when he was sent away. His parents died when he was young and there was no one to look after him, so when he got in trouble he was sent away. That's what they did with kids like that in those days.'

'The good old days, how are ye!' Tommy said.

Jack was trying to take all this in.

'What do they do with kids like that these days?' he asked.

'They try to help them I suppose,' Grandad said. 'They have family support and social workers and all sorts nowadays.'

They walked on a little further, the crowd beginning to thin a little as they reached the city centre.

'You know de Valera?' Jack asked.

Tommy and Grandad both stopped and looked at him.

'Johnner doesn't like him very much, does he?'

'No, he doesn't,' Grandad said. 'He played a part in all of the main events leading up to and after the formation of the Irish Republic. He *was* Ireland for us when we were small and for our parents. He fought in 1916 and in the War of Independence and the Civil War. He was the first Taoiseach of the Irish Republic and he wrote the Constitution that we still have today. So he was without doubt the most important man in recent Irish history. But no, Johnner doesn't like him.'

'But why?'

'Ah, for loads of reasons I suppose Jack.' Grandad squinted at the declining sun. 'I suppose he thinks the country and de Valera let him and other people like him down.Jack wasn't sure exactly what Grandad was saying. It seemed to him that people clung onto the bad things much more tightly than they did the good things in life. He was the same himself, he knew. Bad memories and moments of humiliation always came to mind when he felt low, even though he knew that he was lucky compared to so many other kids in the world.

'So de Valera wasn't killed after the Rising?' Jack asked.

'God, he's becoming the right little historian, isn't he Mick?' Tommy said.

'No, he was the only leader to avoid the firing squad,' Grandad said.

'He was lucky,' Jack said.

'I suppose. Some people say he got special treatment. He was an American citizen and Britain wanted America to join the war around that time, so maybe they thought better of shooting him.'

'But he was sent to gaol?'

'God, yes.'

'For how long?'

Grandad looked at Tommy.

'I don't know, a few years maybe,' Grandad said.

'No, I think he only did about a year or so because he was elected as an MP in 1918.' Tommy was pleased with himself. He winked at Jack. 'Him and Johnner think they're the only ones who know anything about our history.'

Chapter 11

Jack was lying in his own bed in Islington looking up at his Arsenal poster on the wall. His mother was calling him down to breakfast, but there was none of the usual anxiety of a school day morning in her voice. It must have been the holidays. He closed his eyes, pulled the duvet up to his chin and settled down deep into his comfortable bed. It seemed like a long time since he and his mum spent a lazy morning together. She always seemed to be at work these days and when she was at home she was forever taking calls or answering emails.

The doorbell rang, but she did not answer it at first. It rang a few more times before the door was opened and Jack heard a familiar male voice. It was Matt! He hadn't realised how much he missed him. They could go to the park later, maybe play some football. But there was another voice too, an older man's voice. After a moment Jack knew who it was. It was Grandad.

He opened his eyes. The Arsenal team were nowhere to be seen; they had been replaced by cream wallpaper that peeled back from an off-white ceiling. The familiar smell of damp assaulted his senses. It was awful. The dream had seemed so real.

Then the voices came up to him again, clear enough, but the words were indistinct. He jumped out of bed and opened his door. It was Matt alright, but what was he doing here? He waited to hear his mother's voice, but he could only hear Matt and Grandad talking. Jack's mind began to race then, imagining where his mum could be. Perhaps she had sent Matt to bring him home.

He crept out onto the landing, leaned over the railing and saw Matt standing in the hall. He was overtaken by an urge to go to him and so he ran downstairs and threw his arms around his stepfather.

'Matt, Matt, you came to get me!' He hoped that Grandad wouldn't take this expression of a desire to leave as a slight. Matt laughed.

'Jack, it's great to see you too at last. I've missed you mate. Kate tells me you're having great fun with your grandad.'

The mention of his mum's name only highlighted the strange fact that she was the only one who wasn't present, and the one who should have been.

Jack wanted to know when he would be going home, but he was afraid to come right out and ask because of Grandad. Standing beside Matt he looked old, and kind of sad also. Perhaps, Jack guessed, it was because he would be leaving soon. They'd had a fun time together, all in all, once Jack had gotten used to the place. It would be sad to be leaving on one level.

Grandad finally spoke.

'Come on in Matt and have some breakfast. You're probably tired, you must have had an early start.'

The three of them sat around Grandad's poky kitchen table and ate buttered toast and drank tea.

'This is new Jack,' Matt said. 'I never saw you drinking tea before.'

Jack smiled.

'I've learned lots of new things since I came here Matt, haven't I Grandad?'

'You sure have Jack. We went to see the Dubs yesterday.'

'The Dubs?' Matt asked.

'The Dublin Gaelic Football team,' Grandad said.

'It's really good Matt,' Jack said, 'really fast – and tough too!'

'Can't be as good as the Arsenal though, eh?' Matt smiled.

'No, of course not, but really good all the same.'

All the time they talked Jack kept wondering about his mum. Why was nobody mentioning her? He couldn't help himself.

'When is Mum coming?'

Matt and Grandad looked at each other. After a moment Matt turned to him and put his hand on his arm.

'Jack, I don't want you to worry, okay. Kate isn't feeling well at the moment. She hasn't been well for some time and she's been hiding it from you and from me. But she's in the hospital now which is good. She's getting some tests done. There's nothing to worry about, okay? That's why she can't be here with us now. She asked me to come over and see you, to tell you how much she loves you and that she'll be with you very soon.'

Jack was looking down while Matt spoke and when he finished he looked up at Grandad's face. The sadness he saw there was just too much and he jumped up from the table and ran upstairs to his room and threw himself onto his bed. He wished he was at home; he was cross with his mother for not being here, for being sick, for turning his whole world upside down. And as he lay on his bed crying, thinking these things, he felt sorry for himself. It was useless. He grew angry with himself then for being so selfish, for being a burden on his mother all the time, for not being able to do anything for himself or by himself.

After a while there was a soft knock on the door and Grandad came into the room. He sat on the edge of the bed and Jack could hear his breath coming quick and shallow. He did not speak and after a moment Jack lifted his face from the damp pillow and turned to him.

'I'm sorry for crying, Grandad,' he said.

'Don't be sorry Jack. Crying is good. We all do it.'

Jack couldn't imagine Grandad ever crying. He had looked through old photos with him and he had always seemed such a strong man. Now he wondered.

'Don't ever be afraid to cry,' Grandad said. 'Please God your mam will be okay soon and you'll be back with her where you belong. I know it's not been easy for you coming here.'

'No, no, Grandad. I've loved it here. I love it here.'

'Matt can take you home now if you prefer. He can look after you until your mam is well again.'

Jack didn't know what to say. This was all he had wanted since he came here, to go back home to his friends and school, to get away from this peculiar place where the past seemed to live on in the present. Now he wasn't so sure.

'Do I have to go today?' he asked.

'No, not at all. You don't have to go until you're ready to. I'm only glad to have you here with me,' Grandad said.

Jack didn't want to think about it anymore.

'I want to stay with you Grandad,' he said, 'until Mum is well again. Can I stay with you?'

'Of course you can son, of course you can.' And he hugged Jack for a long time to try to hide the tears that had begun to fill his eyes.

Jack was crying again too. When Grandad released him from the hug Jack sat up on the bed.

'She'll be okay, won't she Grandad?'

'Don't worry Jack, she'll be fine, I promise you.'

But Jack knew that Grandad couldn't make a promise like that. He kept thinking of how his grandmother had died. Huntington's Disease. When he was at the library with Grandad the day before he found a medical dictionary and looked it up. He couldn't understand a lot of it but he knew that hereditary meant it runs in families. And he knew that Grandad must have known that too.

Matt had brought some school books with him and some assignments that Jack's teachers had set for him, but Jack had no interest in even looking at them. Usually he worked very hard at school and tried his best to get good grades. Now his books looked strange to him, as if they belonged to another boy and not him. He tried to think about his school and friends, but he couldn't even picture his best friend Jason's face.

Later that day, after Matt had left to go back to the airport, Peadar called around to see him. He was quiet still, thinking of his mother by herself in some strange smelling hospital ward, missing him no doubt. He knew nothing about hospitals beyond one visit he made to casualty with Matt when he thought he might have fractured a wrist after falling in the playground. It was only heavy bruising, but the endless wait and the crowds and the peculiar smells had made a bad impression on him.

Grandad let Peadar in and he came up to Jack's room and found him reading a book he'd borrowed from the library on the 1916 Rising. There were lots of old black and white photos in it of soldiers and rebels and buildings on fire or in ruins. It was just like when he was with Willie, and when Peadar sat next to him to look at it with him, he pointed at a tram and said that he'd seen one just like it.

'Oh in the Transport Museum in Covent Garden? We were there with my Auntie last year,' Peadar said.

'No, I mean I saw one in Dublin,' Jack said.

'Where?'

Jack closed the book and turned to him, his eyes fixed on his.

'Can you keep a secret, Peadar?'

'Of course I can, Jack.'

'You have to promise you won't tell anyone, okay?'

Peadar looked doubtful for a moment.

'You have to promise or I won't tell,' Jack said.

'Okay, I promise.'

'I saw the tram here in Dublin,' Jack said, watching him closely to see his reaction.

'In that dream you were telling me about?' Peadar asked.

Jack nodded. He sensed that his friend doubted him. He figured that he had heard about his mother's illness and Matt's earlier visit and that he more than likely thought that he was not himself. Doubtless Grandad had arranged for his visit in an attempt to lift Jack's spirits in the wake of the bad news.

'Since I came here, I've been having these dreams. No, they're not dreams; they're more than that. Remember I told you about the boy called Willie?' He felt the time had come to tell Peadar everything.

'I remember,' Peadar said, 'go on.'

'When I sleep I go back into the past, to 1916, and the Rising is taking place.'

'Oh Jack, they're only dreams. They're meaningless. All the stuff that's in your head during the day comes out all mixed up in your dreams. That's just the way it is – it doesn't mean anything. Some days I read loads of football books and that night I dream I'm playing for United in the Champions League final. That's how dreams are made. Your grandad and his friends have been filling your head with talk about the Rising, bringing you to the museum and getting these books from the library for you. It's all in there.' Peadar pointed at Jack's head. 'So it all comes out at night when you dream.'

'No, Peadar. It's not like that.' Jack was frustrated, he knew there was something more to it. 'It's real, I know it is.'

Peadar put his hand on his friend's shoulder.

'I heard about your mam,' he said. 'I'm sorry.'

Jack sprung to his feet in anger.

'This has nothing to do with Mum! I'm telling you the truth, but you don't believe me because you think there's something wrong with me. Well there's nothing wrong with me!'

'*Ssh* Jack. I know there's nothing wrong with you, but I know you're worried about your mam. Anybody would be. It's alright,' he said.

'You don't believe me, do you,' Jack said quietly, 'about the Rising?'

'It's not that…'

'But you don't – I know.'

'I believe you're having dreams alright, but I think the reason you're having them is because of all the stuff your Grandad's filling your head with.'

'No, you're wrong Peadar. And I'll prove it,' he said.

Peadar stood up and threw his hands wide apart.

'Okay Jack, let's see you prove it then.'

Jack smiled at him.

'I will,' he said, 'the next time I go back there I'll bring something back with me, something I could only have gotten in 1916. A newspaper or something like that.'

Peadar smiled sadly at him and shook his head.

'I'll believe it when I see it Jack.'

Chapter 12

'Jack! Jack! Are you listening?'

'What? Sorry.'

'You're an awful man, Jack. You were miles away,' Willie said.

'Sorry Willie, what were you saying?' Jack shook his head to clear the cobwebs.

'What do you think of it then? This is where it all starts, the new republic – the GPO.'

Jack looked on as men milled around with guns slung over their shoulders, building up barricades against the windows. In another corner, women in coarse long wool skirts were distributing food to the men.

'It's crazy, Willie. Is your brother here?'

'I see him now alright, over by the far counter,' Willie said pointing and waving.

A handsome young man waved back as he approached them.

'You lads shouldn't be here,' Seán said. 'Things are quiet now, but it won't be like this for long, believe me. Ma will be worried about you Willie, you have to go home.'

Jack could see that Willie was annoyed.

'Just because I'm young! It didn't stop you during the Lockout.'

'I was much older than you are now Willie. Don't have me worried about you, please.' He looked at Jack. 'Make sure he goes home, will you…?'

'Jack, my name is Jack,' Jack said.

'I'm asking you as a favour to me now Jack to make sure he goes home. Will you do that for me?'

'I will,' Jack said.

Willie made a face at him.

'Now, go on. I have things to do. Tell Ma not to be worried, all is well here.'

Seán made his way through the crowd of volunteers across what used to be the main hall of the post office but was now the centre of operations for the Rising.

'We better go,' Jack said.

'*Sssh*. Here he is now!' Willie grabbed Jack's arm tightly.

'Who?'

'Look, it's Pearse.'

A door opened at the rear of the hall and a man in a long army coat emerged and was now striding towards the front of the building. As he walked he was smiling and talking to the men in his charge, stopping every now and again to encourage them, placing a hand on a shoulder here or patting a back there.

A crate was arranged in the middle of the hall and he stood up on it and called the men to listen. As he did so another man came into the hall from a door to the side. He was older with a full, dark moustache and he swung his raincoat from his shoulders and shook it vigorously, creating pools of water on the floor.

'Filthy evening it is now out there,' he said to no one and everyone. Jack was surprised to hear him speak with a strong Scottish accent. The men all turned to smile at him. Jack could tell that he was well liked.

'It's Connolly,' Willie whispered, 'he's been on look-out duty.'

'God help us, he's not making another speech is he?' Connolly said loudly, indicating Pearse with a wave of his hand, a broad smile on his face.

There was a ripple of laughter from the men, but Pearse looked at him blankly.

'I was going to say a few words Jim, if you don't mind too much,' he said.

'Oh don't mind me Pádraig, you work away there.'

The men laughed good-naturedly again and when silence was restored Pearse began to address them. Jack found it hard to understand what he was talking about.

'He has some way with words, doesn't he?' Willie said.

Jack nodded. He certainly did.

When he finished the men all clapped and cheered. Stacks of papers were brought out and given to some of the women from Cumann na mBan to distribute.

Willie hurried over to where the papers were and grabbed a handful.

'Come on with me,' he said, 'we have another job to do!'

'What is it?' Jack asked, indicating the pages.

'It's a manifesto.'

'What's a manifesto?'

'What he just said, you gombeen!' Willie threw his eyes up to heaven. 'Come on!'

Jack followed him to a door at the rear where an armed volunteer let them out onto the street. The first darkening of evening was apparent in the air outside. Jack grabbed Willie by the arm.

'Here let me read it first!' he said.

Willie took a copy off the top of the bundle and handed it to Jack. This is what it said:

THE PROVISIONAL GOVERNMENT
To The CITIZENS OF DUBLIN

The Provisional Government of the Irish Republic salutes the Citizens of Dublin on the momentous occasion of the proclamation of a SOVEREIGN INDEPENDENT IRISH STATE, now in course of being established by Irishmen in arms.

The Republican forces hold the lines taken up at twelve noon on Easter Monday, and nowhere, despite fierce and almost continuous attacks of the British troops, have the lines been broken through. The country is rising in answer to Dublin's call, and the final achievement of Ireland's freedom is now, with God's help, only a matter of days. The valour, self-sacrifice and discipline of Irish men and women are about to win for our country a glorious place among the nations.

Ireland's honour has already been redeemed; it remains to vindicate her wisdom and her self-control. All citizens of Dublin who believe in the right of their country to be free will give their allegiance and their loyal help to the Irish Republic. There is work for everyone: for the men in the fighting line, and for the women in the provision of food and first aid. Every Irishman and Irishwoman worthy of the name will come forward to help their common country in this her supreme hour. Able-bodied citizens can help by building barricades in the streets to oppose the advance of the British troops. The British troops have been firing on our women and on our Red Cross. On the other hand, Irish Regiments in the British Army have refused to act against their fellow-countrymen.

The Provisional Government hopes that its supporters which means the vast bulk of the people of Dublin—will preserve order and self-restraint. Such looting as has already occurred has been done by hangers-on of the British Army. Ireland must keep her new honour unsmirched. We have lived to see an Irish Republic proclaimed. May we live to establish it firmly, and may our children and our children's children enjoy the happiness and prosperity which freedom will bring.

Signed on behalf of the Provisional Government,

P. H. PEARSE,

Commanding in Chief of the Forces of the Irish Republic, and President of the Provisional Government.

When he had finished reading Jack folded the sheet of paper and stuffed it in his pocket.

'You have to go home now Willie,' Jack said. 'I promised your brother.'

'Would you go on out a that! We have work to do Jack. We must take copies of the manifesto all around the city, to let people know about the success of the rising.'

'Come on Willie, you heard your brother. It's too dangerous for us to be out tonight. It will be dark in no time at all.'

'Don't worry about that. No one will harm us Jack, we're just children. The British Army won't be shooting at us!'

'But I promised Seán.'

'I know, but it's for the new republic – and we'll go straight home when we're finished. Alright?'

'I suppose.'

They headed off down Sackville Street toward the river past the Metropole Hotel. The windows of Clerys and other shops along the street had been broken and people were openly looting. A large group of children were milling around the destroyed front window of a toyshop further on, some emerging with boxes of toys and fireworks under their arms.

'It's not really like he says in the manifesto, is it Willie?' Jack said, looking over at the kids, one of whom had cut his hand on broken glass and was shrieking loudly while his older brother shouted at him to go home.

'Don't mind them. There's always people who are only ever out to help themselves,' Willie replied.

Willie planned to take copies of the manifesto to all of the main outposts of the Rising starting with Jacob's Factory. When they crossed the bridge over the river something caught Jack's eye.

'Look!'

Willie stopped and followed the line of Jack's finger as it pointed east along the river. A huge British Navy Gunboat was slowly approaching the Customs House along the quays.

'Come on quickly!' Willie said, and he ran off up Westmoreland Street.

Before long they reached Jacob's, but there was no answer when they knocked. A voice hissed down to them from an upstairs window. Willie made himself known and waved the manifestos as proof of his story. The garrison was nervous it seemed; all day they had been receiving abuse from passing members of the public and for a while a large group had gathered outside taunting them.

A ladder was lowered from above and Willie and Jack began to climb up. As they neared the window Jack looked back over his shoulder in the direction of the GPO and he saw beautiful red and green and golden flames fly up, illuminating Nelson on his column. He knew it was just the kids with the fireworks they had stolen, but he knew also that there would be much worse to come before the week was over. He forced himself to look away, but the colours stayed with him and swirled. His head grew light and he was falling.

'Jack!' Willie shouted.

Chapter 13

When he woke he was lying on the hard bedroom floor. His legs were bound together in the twisted tartan blanket and his arms were stretched out in front of him as if he had attempted to break his fall. His attempt was only partially successful because he could feel a throbbing pain in his left temple where he had struck his head against the bedside locker. A thin smear of blood covered his palm when he rubbed his eyes and took his hand away.

He could hear the radio downstairs, and his grandad rattling around the kitchen making tea, talking to himself. But no, there was another voice, a lighter voice also. He heard quick footsteps on the stairs and realised that they were not his grandfather's. The door flew open then.

'Jack O'Connor! You're the laziest boy I know,' Sally shouted at him. But she was smiling too.

Jack reddened. He was mortified. How could they let Sally find him here lying on his bedroom floor in his old pyjamas?

'Did you fall out of bed?'

'What do you think?' Jack was sullen, still partially living in the world he had just left, unsure of his new reality. He was confused a lot these days because he found both his sleeping and waking lives equally perplexing.

'Someone's not a morning person I can tell,' Sally said. 'Come on and get dressed and have some breakfast. Your grandad has some stuff to do today so I'm in charge.'

She skipped back down the stairs then and Jack awkwardly unwrapped the blanket from his legs so that he could stand up. He wondered where Grandad was going. It was obviously important because he must have arranged in advance for Sally to come over and keep an eye on him.

He went to the bathroom and splashed some cold water on his face. Back in his room he spent more time than usual picking out his clothes and putting on deodorant; he even combed his unruly hair, parting it to one side. He made his bed quickly and, folding his pyjamas, he felt something unusual in the trouser pocket. It was a piece of paper folded twice. He sat down on the bed and opened it slowly, his heartbeat quickening. The room began to spin, his eyes unfocused. He closed his eyes for a moment and opened them again.

It was the manifesto.

Sally called out his name from below, once and then again. He couldn't stand up. He tried to force himself to breathe deeply, but instead he drew in air in short, shallow breaths. It was all real then after all. He had really been there, and this would prove it.

He folded up the page again and stuffed it in the pocket of his jeans. He went to the window and looked down on the street below. Rain fell steadily on a long line of parked cars. He heard the front door open.

'Don't be all day up there Jack!' Grandad called up to him. 'Have a lovely day with Sally and Peadar, and remember Sally's in charge. I'll see you later on this evening.'

The front door closed, and from his vantage point Jack watched Grandad open an umbrella and walk down the street. Dressed up in a suit and raincoat he looked different, dapper, most unlike himself. The day hadn't started for Jack and already it had taken a strange turn.

Sally had their day planned out. They took the bus to town and marched up Grafton Street towards St. Stephens' Green amid a crowd of shoppers. They passed mimes and musicians playing all styles of music, and there were beggars too, sitting in the damp doorways of shops, paper cups in front of them with scribbled cardboard signs asking for money. Jack enjoyed the music, but he tried not to look at the faces of the men and women who begged. It was impossible. His eyes were drawn to their pleading eyes and he noticed also how their hands were dirty, the nails bitten to the quick, the knuckles red and sore.

He walked alongside Peadar in Sally's wake. She appeared to take her role of minder seriously, feigning maturity and keeping aloof.

'Let's look around the shops first and then we'll get something to eat,' she said.

Jack nodded. He was happy to be out of the house and Peadar was good company. As they walked and browsed he wondered about Sally. She must be bored looking after him and Peadar. He watched her as she walked beside him; she was so pretty. He imagined himself in the near future telling Jason and his other friends in London about her. How would he describe her? Good-looking, tough and sometimes a little scary, but someone you could trust, he thought. He began to think of London, but any thoughts of there were spoiled now by worries about his mum and his future. Yet he was still here in Dublin, and by his own choice. He felt guilty now for choosing to stay with Grandad. No matter where he was or what he was doing he always felt that he should be somewhere else, doing something else. An invisible thread was pulling him away from where he was and what he was doing. It was hard to explain. He knew he should be happy to be out with Peadar and Sally without any adults to interfere in their fun, but he did not feel happy.

After half an hour in the Stephen's Green Shopping Centre Sally turned to him.

'Okay, what's wrong with you Jack?'

'Nothing.'

'Don't give me that! You've been moping around all morning. Is it your mam?'

The mere mention of her name these days made Jack want to cry, but of course that was unthinkable in front of Sally. He put his hand in his pocket and pinched his thigh hard. He felt the manifesto, smooth against his fingertips. He remembered Pearse's speech to the garrison and this gave him some courage.

'I heard she was sick,' Sally went on. 'Your grandad told me.'

'But she'll be well again soon,' Peadar said.

'Yes, and then you can go home again back to your precious London. But for now you're stuck here with us.'

Jack said nothing. He couldn't understand why Sally was being so mean to him.

'He likes it here, don't you Jack?' Peadar asked.

Jack nodded.

'See?' Peadar said to Sally. He turned back to Jack. 'Your grandad told us you wanted to stay here with him. Is that true?

That your stepdad was going to take you back to London, but you said you'd prefer to stay here.'

'That's right,' Jack said.

'Why?' Sally asked, and she gave him a very peculiar look.

'I don't know,' he said. 'It's just different here I suppose. I feel different here. Do you know what I mean?'

'I think so,' Peadar said.

Sally threw her eyes up to heaven and took him by the hand and led him towards the door of the shopping centre.

'I can tell you're not a shopper. Am I right?' she asked.

'Yeah.'

They walked slowly along Grafton Street for a while.

'Remember we were talking the other day about 1916?' Jack said to Peadar.

'What's all this about 1916?' Sally asked.

Peadar and Jack exchanged a look.

'You might as well tell her,' Jack said.

'Tell me what?' Sally asked.

'It's nothing. Just that Jack has been having these strange dreams since he came to Dublin.'

'Strange how?'

'They're not dreams!' Jack interjected.

'Well, he goes to sleep and then he's back in 1916, during the Rising – '

'Oh come on! It's no wonder the way your grandad goes on about it!' Sally said.

'That's what I said,' Peadar chimed in.

'Well I was back there again last night,' Jack announced.

Sally stopped and looked at him. All around them shoppers, laden down with bags, passed them by.

'And?' Sally asked.

'It's real,' he said. 'I know it is.'

'What's real? What are you on about?' She turned to her brother. 'What's he on about?'

'He thinks his dreams are real,' Peadar said patiently.

'For the last time Peadar, they're not dreams!' Jack said. 'And I can prove it.'

Sally was standing looking at him with her mouth open. Jack thought she looked funny, most unlike her usually perfect self.

'You're starting to freak me out now Jack,' Peadar said. 'You better stop it, do you hear me?'

'Okay,' Jack said. 'Let's get something to eat – my treat. And then we'll visit the museum. I've got something to show you.'

They ate in a fast food restaurant and then jumped on a tram up to the museum. The rain had eased off as they walked across the courtyard towards the main entrance.

Jack turned to Peadar and Sally and smiled.

'What are you smiling at?' Sally asked.

'You two,' he said happily. 'Before we go inside I'm going to show you something incredible, okay?'

Jack took the folded piece of paper from his pocket and handed it to Sally and Peadar. He waited patiently while they read it.

'So what? It's just a copy of an old document.' Sally said, before she'd finished reading.

'Yes,' Jack said, 'but how did I get it?'

'I don't know, do I?' There was a note of impatience in her voice.

'You could have downloaded it from the internet,' Peadar chimed in.

'Grandad doesn't have a computer, let alone a printer.' Jack smiled at them. 'Come with me,' he said, leading them to the door.

Inside they made their way to the Rising Exhibition area where Jack showed them a glass case containing many official documents. There was a copy of Chief of Staff, Eoin MacNeill's order cancelling the Rising from the Irish Independent on Easter Sunday; there was a copy of the Proclamation of the Irish Republic signed by the seven leaders of the Rising, and then there was a copy of the manifesto signed by Pearse. Jack opened out his copy and laid it on the glass beside the museum copy.

'See?' he said.

'Yes I see,' Sally said. 'It's a copy of the one they have here. Big deal – ' Sally turned away and idly examined another exhibit.

'No, you don't get it!' Jack's eyes opened wide as he looked at Peadar. 'I brought this back with me from 1916.'

Peadar began to shake his head slowly.

'No Jack. No. That's not even funny.'

'But it's true! I swear it!'

Peadar looked at him like there was something wrong with him. Jack was sorry he'd shown it to them; he wondered why he just couldn't be like any other normal kid and simply get on with his life. He hadn't asked for any of this to happen to him. He never wanted to come here. He never wanted his mother to get sick. He never even thought of himself as Irish up until now, and here he was trying to convince his friends that he was somehow travelling back one hundred years through time in his sleep. This was his breaking point. It was all too much for him.

He pounded his closed fist against the glass case, making Peadar flinch. Before he knew it a blazered attendant was beside him.

'You can't do that young man!' the attendant said. 'These documents are fragile.'

'I... I'm sorry,' Jack mumbled.

'What's that you have there?' The man took the manifesto from Jack's hand. 'Hey, how did you get hold of this? Stay there and don't move,' he said, and then he spoke into his radio: 'Can you send someone over straight away John? We have an attempted theft from the collection here. See can you get the Guards on this ASAP.'

Sally appeared behind the attendant and simply mouthed the word "run" at Jack and Peadar. All three took off and as they did Sally pulled the manifesto from the attendant's hand and it tore from top to bottom. This seemed to cause the man some distress, enough to allow Sally, Peadar and Jack an opportunity to put some distance between them before he could alert security to block the exit doors. Soon they were out in the courtyard and then out on the street and they ran all the way to Heuston station where they stopped to rest, safe among the crowd.

'Show me what you have left?' Jack asked.

Sally held up the torn sheet and Jack took it back from her.

'Do you believe that it's real now?' Jack asked.

Sally simply shook her head and walked away.

'I don't know what to believe,' Peadar said, 'but that fella seemed to think it was real enough to call the Guards over.

Chapter 14

By the time they got home it was late afternoon and Grandad had not yet returned from wherever it was he had gone. Rather than leave him on his own, Sally and Peadar took Jack back to their house where Mrs. Morrison made them tea and sandwiches. She sat with them at the small kitchen table, but she didn't eat anything herself. Instead she smoked cigarette after cigarette and smiled at Jack, her head tilted to one side.

'Do you like Dublin Jack?' she asked.

'Yes I do Mrs. Morrison.'

'You're a lovely polite young man Jack,' she said, puffing on her cigarette. 'Isn't he Sally?'

Sally rolled her eyes.

'Will you leave him alone Mam and let him have his tea in peace?' Peadar said.

'I'm not bothering you Jack, am I?'

'Not at all, Mrs. Morrison,' Jack replied.

'Do you hear that– *not at all Mrs. Morrison*! Isn't he something else?' She gave her children a meaningful look. Her son smiled at her, but her daughter sighed loudly, put her elbows on the table and held her head in her hands.

'I remember your mother well,' Mrs. Morrison went on. 'We were at school together – she was a few years ahead of me of course.'

To Jack she looked much older than his mother.

'Well, primary school only. Kate went to an expensive boarding school down the country somewhere I think. We just went to the nuns up the road for our secondary. I remember the first summer she came home, she was like a little lady. She spoke with a beautiful accent, much like your own Jack.'

'You knew my grandmother too then?' Jack said.

'Oh yes, Mrs. O'Connor was a lovely woman. I'm sure she came from money too. Your grandad did well to land her I think, and he knew it. He worshipped the ground she walked on.'

'She died young,' Jack said without looking up.

Mrs. Morrison paused for a moment before she replied, as if considering for a moment if it were appropriate to tackle such a dark subject with the boy.

'Yes, she did,' she said at last. 'She was far too young to die.'

'It was Huntington's Disease, wasn't it?' Jack wanted more information.

'Yes, I believe it was.' A note of hesitation had crept into Mrs. Morrison's voice.

'That's enough of that,' Sally cut in. 'It's depressing. Let's go and see if your grandad has come home yet.'

'Let him finish his tea Sally,' Mrs. Morrison said. 'It's only natural that he wants to learn more about his family.' She smiled at Jack again.

He ate in silence for a moment while all three of them watched his every move. When he had finished eating, he added another spoonful of sugar to his tea and stirred it hard before swallowing a large mouthful.

'My mother is in hospital,' he said. He wasn't sure why he was saying this, but he felt the need to talk about her and Mrs. Morrison seemed happy to listen. Grandad had hardly mentioned her illness since Matt went back to London. Still he found it hard to make eye contact with any of them. He watched the tea swirl in his mug.

'I'm sorry son, I didn't know.' Mrs. Morrison said quietly. 'Is she alright?'

'I don't know,' Jack said. 'She's having tests done. Matt says that she'll be fine, she just needs time.'

'I'm really sorry Jack,' she said again.

She opened up the biscuit tin in front of her and offered Jack another chocolate biscuit, as if that would make everything better.

Jack didn't take one, even though he would have liked one. He didn't want to look up in case his eyes met Mrs. Morrison's. There was a wobble in her voice that signified emotion, and he knew that he would end up crying if she did, and he didn't want to cry in front of Peadar and Sally.

'Who's Matt?' Mrs. Morrison asked after a few moments, realising that this was a name she was unfamiliar with. She closed the biscuit tin before her children could take a second biscuit.

'He's my stepdad.'

'Come on Jack, Peadar, we should go.' Sally stood up.

'You can't go now Sally. Can you not see the boy's upset?'

'Yes, of course I can – it's you who's upset him!'

'Don't be ridiculous girl! I didn't upset you Jack, did I?' Mrs. Morrison asked.

'No, not at all.' Jack's eyes were still fixed on the table in front of him.

'His grandad's bound to be home by now, and he'll be wondering where we are,' Peadar said, shoving his chair back.

Within a few moments Peadar had bundled him out to the front door and Sally had gone to fetch their jackets. Jack could hear mother and daughter exchanging urgent whispered words at the end of the hall while he waited at the threshold with Peadar. He knew what they were saying even though he couldn't make out the words exactly. It had to do with illness and his mother and his grandmother. Mrs. Morrison mentioned Grandad and how sad it was for him, just when he got his daughter back he was losing her again.

Sally shut the door firmly in their wake. She had not said goodbye to her mother either. She was cross, Jack could tell, but he wasn't sure if it was him or her mother who was the cause of it. No one spoke until they were almost at Grandad's house.

'Don't mind Mam, Jack,' Peadar said. 'She's means well, but she can be awful silly sometimes.'

Jack wasn't sure what to say. He wasn't annoyed at Mrs. Morrison. He just felt very lost. Sally stopped suddenly and turned to him.

'I'm sorry Jack. You're having a horrible time of it.'

She put her arms around him there on the street and held him close. It was too much. The heartfelt sympathy of this tough girl was more than he could bear. He started to cry, little sobs at first but soon he was bawling like a baby. He couldn't stop himself once he got started.

Peadar searched in his pockets and found a tissue for him. They walked him around the streets for a while until he felt better.

'Don't let your grandad see that you've been crying,' Sally said. 'He'll only be upset.'

'We're here for you Jack, no matter what,' Peadar whispered.

Jack nodded, and Sally rang the bell.

Grandad looked very tired when he opened the door. It was as if Jack hadn't seen him for years. It was like that story Grandad had told him about Oisín coming back from Tír na nÓg, falling from his horse and aging in a moment. Time had caught up with Grandad too it seemed; in just one day he had become very old.

Jack said goodbye to Peadar and Sally at the door before he followed Grandad inside.

'Thanks Peadar, thanks Sally. Will you call for me tomorrow again?' he asked.

'For sure!' Peadar said.

He watched them walk off down the road and then Grandad closed the front door softly. They stood for a moment in the evening gloom of the hall.

'I have someone I want you to meet now Jack. Are you okay?'

Jack nodded.

He was not surprised when he walked into the living room and saw Robert sitting on the sofa. He had never admitted it of course, but he knew from the first that there was something that tied him to that nervous young man. Robert sprung to his feet and smiled at him sheepishly. Grandad stood behind Jack with one hand placed lightly on his shoulder.

'Jack,' he said, 'you remember Robert of course? Robert, here, is your half-brother.'

Robert continued to smile, but Jack said nothing. He felt Grandad's hand squeeze his shoulder and he took it to mean that he was expected to say something. But he found he could not say anything at all. It was as if he was struck dumb. While he wasn't surprised by what Grandad had said, at the same time it was the last thing he expected to hear him say.

'This is hard,' Grandad went on. 'It's hard for all of us to take in.' He looked at Robert. 'You've obviously known this for some time, but for us, well it's going to take a little while to get used to.'

Jack wanted to leave the room. He wanted to run upstairs to his bed, wrap himself up in the blankets and go to sleep. But even in sleep there was no escape from the world. Bad things happened no matter where he was. He wished he could go back in time to when he was happy. When had that been? Before he came to Dublin? Before his mum got sick? Before she and Matt started to argue? He wasn't sure. Had he ever been happy, even in London?

'I hope we can be friends Jack,' Robert said, and he put out his hand.

Jack looked at it, the pale skin, the long thin fingers, and he thought of his mother's delicate hands. It was true. She was his mother too. He wanted to scream, but he didn't.

He took Robert's hand in his and shook it, but still he could not say a thing. He turned to Grandad then.

'I think I'll go to upstairs now Grandad. I'm tired.'

'You must be hungry, have some supper with us first,' Grandad said. 'No thanks, Mrs. Morrison gave me my tea. I'm just tired.'

He turned and said goodnight quickly over his shoulder, but not before he noted Robert's face; how he bit his lower lip and looked away.

He ran upstairs and shut his bedroom door behind him, kicked off his trainers and climbed into bed. He did not want to think about anything. He wanted only to fall asleep. He didn't want to dream either. After a while he dozed, but woke with a start. The house was quiet. He felt cold now in his clothes with the blankets around him. He reached down to the foot of the bed and pulled his grandmother's tartan blanket up around him to keep himself warm.

Chapter 15

He opened his eyes slowly. His vision was blurred. A child's face, grubby with rosy cheeks and big wondering eyes gazed down into his. A woman's voice called out from a little way off.

'Leave the boy alone, Michael!'

The face disappeared and Jack tried to sit up. His head was sore and he felt a bit dizzy as he straightened himself up. Willie appeared now out of the gloom carrying a steaming bowl and spoon. Jack sat up in the bed, which was not really a bed so much as a wooden pallet covered by a thin mattress and some blankets.

'Ah you're awake at last Jack. I was worried about you for a while there,' Willie said.

'What happened?' Jack asked.

'You don't remember?'

'No.'

'Here, have some soup and I'll tell you.'

Willie straightened up the bed and set the soup bowl down in front of Jack.

'We were climbing up into Jacob's and you fell from the ladder,' he said.

'I remember now Willie. I was watching the fireworks and I missed my step. I don't remember anything after that.'

'They took you into Jacob's and a nice woman from Cumann na mBan looked after you. Then I borrowed a barrow from Georges Street market and wheeled you home.'

'Is that where we are then, your home?' Jack asked.

'This is it Jack.' Willie threw his arms open wide as if to indicate that all this splendour was his.

The room was divided into sections by drawn curtains and was cramped with old mismatched furniture. The walls were filthy with damp and heavy old paper peeled away from the corners. There was only one small window, which was barred on the outside and gave very little light. It was hard to tell if it was morning, noon or night. A woman appeared in the doorway then. She was thin and tired looking, but she was also beautiful, or had been at one time in the past.

'So how are you feeling, Jack?' she asked.

'I'm fine, thanks.' He smiled and the woman placed a hand on Willie's shoulder.

'Willie will bring you home later when you feel better. I know your grandfather must be worried about you, the way things are at the moment. Eat up your soup now and get your strength back young man.'

Jack held the spoon in his right hand. The soup looked clear and greasy and not at all appetising. He lifted a small amount to his lips and tasted it. It was hot and salty and tasted good and he took another spoonful. Each mouthful provoked a thirst for more and in a matter of minutes the bowl was empty.

'Would you like some more?' Willie's mother asked.

Jack was just about to say yes when he noticed two small children peeping around the heavy curtains at him.

'No, no thanks, Mrs. Mahon, that was lovely. I'm full up now.' He didn't want to take any more of the scarce food from these poor people.

When Willie and Jack were left alone, Willie began to fill him in on the latest developments. All morning the gunboat that they had seen on the Liffey the night before had been shelling Liberty Hall. Luckily the place was empty by then and there were no casualties.

'You live right beside the GPO, don't you?' Jack asked.

'Yeah, near enough. Why?'

'You and your family will be in danger when they start shelling the GPO,' he said.

Willie laughed. 'They won't do that Jack. I was in there this morning with Seán and they said the British would never destroy their own Post Office – never mind all the businesses in the area that would be in danger. The cost would be too much for them to bear.'

Jack thought of all the photographs he'd seen in the museum of Sackville Street in ruins. He had to convince Willie of the real danger his family were in.

'All the same Willie,' he said, 'one way or another the British will come here and it would be better for you and your family if you were somewhere far away when that happens.'

'I'm not running away Jack – I'm no coward!'

'I know you're not,' Jack said, 'but think of your mum and the little ones.'

Willie stood for a while rubbing his chin in thought as if he had a beard there.

'Maybe,' he said after a while. 'Let's have a look around outside first. Are you able to get up?'

Jack struggled to his feet. His head was sore, but he felt alright. He followed Willie through the house, past other curtained rooms, each one more crowded than the last until they came to a rotten wooden door. Willie dragged it open and stepped outside and Jack followed, stumbling as he went, disoriented by the sudden sunlight. He had not realised just how dark it was inside. He stopped for a moment and was struck by how quiet it was too. He followed Willie onto Moore Street and then onto Henry Street. There was no one about. The shops were all shut.

'Has the city closed down completely?' Jack asked.

'Not entirely,' Willie laughed, 'the pubs are still open.'

They were approaching the Post Office now and still there was no sign of any life. Jack could hear a strange whistling sound and the boys stopped and turned to each other.

'Oh my God!' Willie cried and he dragged Jack back up Henry Street just as the first shell exploded.

'They're shelling Sackville Street!' Willie shouted. 'I can't believe they're shelling their own!'

'Just keep moving!' Jack shouted back.

They ran on until they came to the markets and all the while the shells kept coming.

'I have to go back,' Willie said. 'A stray shell could kill everyone at home. You stay here and wait for me.'

'I'm going with you Willie. I want to help if I can.'

They ran back the way they had just come, the sound of the explosions getting louder as they came. It seemed such a strange thing to do, Jack thought as he ran, to run towards the bombs. But he was not afraid. He could not explain it. He knew this was real – just as real as his other life with

Grandad – but he had no care for his safety. It was not that he felt invincible in this world. He was worn out. He felt tired as he ran. Not just in the physical sense, but tired of trying to understand things, tired of worrying about the future. For the moment he was prepared to simply let what might happen happen; he had not got the strength to do anything else.

When they got back to Moore Street there was chaos. Hundreds of men, women and children were milling about on the street. Willie's mother had gathered up her children and whatever belongings they could carry and were already out on the street. She hugged Willie close when they ran up to her and Jack felt her love for her son so sharply it was like a knife to his heart. All this time he had been trying not to think about his mother, doing all he could to exist in whatever alien present he happened to find himself in, but now it was too much. He felt her love in that moment, in the protective embrace of another mother for another son. He had grown up so much in this past week, but now he was done with learning and with growing. He wanted everything to stop. He looked at Willie's little sister and brothers as they held on to their mother's skirts and he wanted to be like them, he wanted be a child again.

Mrs. Mahon had taken a basket with some food and clothes with her and from this basket she produced a woollen blanket which she drew around her shoulders. She picked up Willie's little sister then and wrapped her in it carefully before they set off walking.

'Come on Jack, quickly!'

Willie called to Jack who was distracted. The blanket was exactly like the one his grandmother had, the one he wrapped himself in to get to sleep at night.

Willie had an aunt in Cuckoo Lane at the back of the Jameson distillery and he and Jack went that far with his mother before heading back to the river towards Kingsbridge Station. They passed the Royal Barracks which Jack recognised as the museum he and Grandad had visited. Jack was still thinking about his mother and his new step-brother and, consumed by his own worries, he forgot about Willie and his family's safety.

They looked back along the river as they crossed King's Bridge and they could see smoke rising black and grey above buildings in the distance. Willie was quiet as they walked.

'Are you worried about Seán?' Jack asked.

'He knows what he's doing, I'm not worried about him,' Willie said.

'But your mum, she must be worried about him?'

'She knows that he's doing the right thing.'

'Are you sure about that Willie?' Jack asked.

'Course I'm sure.'

'She looks worried and sad to me,' Jack said.

Willie turned to him then. He was stern and looked much older than his twelve years.

'That's the way people look in the real world Jack,' he said, and he turned on his heel.

'Here, come back! What does that mean?' Jack was annoyed with his friend.

'It means we're different, that's all.'

'That's not my fault, is it?' Jack defended himself.

'No. I'm sorry. I'm not getting at you Jack. I don't know your story, but you're obviously well off and you don't have to worry about money or food or stuff like that. But for us it's different – that's all I'm saying. Da died last year in an accident at the docks and Mam is always sick because she has to work all the time and she never gets a rest and the little ones are sick because they don't get enough to eat, but that's not your problem.'

Jack was getting more and more annoyed as he listened to Willie's lecture.

'I'm sorry Willie. But you know nothing about me or my life – nothing at all! My mother is sick too, in fact she's probably dying. That's why I'm stuck here with my grandad.'

Willie's mouth opened wide, but no words came out.

Jack was on the verge of tears.

'And my dad is dead too! At least you got to know yours. Mine died when I was just a baby.'

It was Jack's turn to storm off now and Willie gave chase after a moment.

'I'm sorry Jack, I didn't know!' he called after him.

'It doesn't matter!' Jack shouted back to him. 'It doesn't matter! Nothing matters anymore!'

He ran off on his own up the hill in what he hoped was the direction of Grandad's house.

Chapter 16

Jack seemed to be walking for hours. He hardly took notice of the city and its inhabitants as they passed him by. Without looking up at all he somehow found his way back to Haroldville Avenue. He had so many things on his mind it was impossible to focus on any one thing for any amount of time. When he rang the front doorbell he was not surprised to find Grandad standing in front of him. He looked worried.

'Are you sleepwalking again Jack?' he asked.

'No Grandad. I just went out for some air and I locked myself out.'

Grandad ushered him in quickly.

'It's not safe, you know. I'm going to have to lock that door from the inside and hide the key I think.'

'Has he gone then?' Jack asked.

'If you mean Robert, then yes he has. He stayed for a bit last night after you went up to bed. I think he was hoping you would come back downstairs.'

Jack went to the kitchen and flicked the switch on the kettle.

'Did you have breakfast yet Grandad?' he asked.

'I did,' Grandad said. 'I wasn't sure whether to wake you or not. You were very quiet last night.'

Jack sat down at the kitchen table. He was tired after walking all over the city all night with Willie. In his heart he knew that it was more than a dream, that it was real; that Willie did exist and he was just as real as Jack was. He'd seen the way Willie worried about his family, he saw the terror in his eyes when the bombs were falling. Jack wished he had been kinder to him before he left him on the street.

'I'm just tired Grandad, that's all,' he said.

Grandad made some tea, hot and sweet, the way they both liked it, and he toasted white bread for Jack which he covered with lots of real butter.

'He wants to get to know you, that's all,' Grandad said.

'I know,' Jack replied, but he wasn't sure he wanted to get to know his brother. Why should he? He meant nothing to Jack. But he was his brother all the same. A brother in name only. There was a long line of questions forming in Jack's mind, but he didn't want to let them develop because he knew that once they did he would have to ask them one by one until he got answers. He feared what those answers would be. Just thinking about Robert made him feel funny, as if he was confined in a tight space without enough air. Every now and again as he chewed his toast he had to stop and gulp down some air. He filled his lungs and held his breath until he had to let it out; it was as if he was on the point of forgetting how to breathe.

'I didn't want to believe it either, that day when he came first.' Grandad went on, determined that he would say his piece. 'I knew, I think, the moment I saw him that he was someone I should know. He has his father's looks, and maybe that's what made me take an instant dislike to him.'

Jack sneaked a quick look at Grandad, but the old man was looking away towards the window. He was too tired to fight the questions anymore.

'Has he spoken to Mum?'

'No, not directly. But they were writing to each other for a while.'

'Is he the reason Mum went away to London all those years ago?'

Grandad didn't answer straight away, and Jack imagined that Grandad was just like his mirror; he too had a long line of answers lining up in his head to match Jack's questions and he dreaded each of those questions being asked, one by one, drawing out the corresponding answer.

'Yes, I suppose,' he said at last. He paused again and Jack imagined him trying out his answers in different formats silently in his mind before he said them out loud. Jack was doing the same thing with his questions. Both wanted the exchange to be over more than anything else in the world and they sought to achieve this with as little upset as possible.

'I don't recognise the man I was then,' Grandad said.

Jack thought he knew what the old man meant, but he prodded nonetheless.

'What do you mean Grandad?'

'I mean, I suppose, that I was very sure of myself and very sure of what was right and what was wrong back then. I'm not like that now, thank God. I didn't like Tony, your mam's boyfriend at the time, and I wasn't slow to let her and him know it.'

'Then Mum had Robert?' Jack asked.

'Yes. But I never knew Robert as a baby.'

'You never knew him?'

'No, he was adopted straight away after the birth.'

'But why couldn't Mum and Tony have kept him?' Jack asked.

'Because Tony wasn't around anymore. To be fair, I suppose I scared him off.' Grandad was looking at the floor.

'So that's why you and Mum never kept in touch?'

'Yes, it was all my fault. I don't know why I was the way I was – it was just the way things were back then.'

Jack didn't want to hear anymore. He didn't want to think of Grandad in this way. He wanted to retreat to his bedroom, use this pause in conversation to escape back to the comfort of his bed, but Grandad wasn't finished yet.

'I'll never forgive myself,' Grandad went on. He looked like he might cry and Jack had to look away. 'It's bad enough what I did to your mam and to little Robert, but when I think of how I added to your grandmother's suffering at the time, it's just too much. She was sick already when we found out Kate was pregnant. Angela would have let them be together, but not me. I was ashamed of them. I was worried what other people might say about us, so I let them take my grandson and then I drove my only child away.'

Now Grandad began to cry quietly to himself. Jack had no idea what to do. He stood up and went to his grandfather and placed his hand on his shoulder. He could feel his body convulse beneath his open palm as the tears came. Jack thought about his mother, all alone in an anonymous hospital in London undergoing tests, and he thought about Willie and his family living in the immediate threat of death and soon tears rolled freely down his cheeks too.

'Ah here, come here,' Grandad said when he saw that Jack was crying, and he hugged his grandson close to him and shushed him. 'It's all a bloody mess right now,' he said, recovering his composure, 'but we can put it right, I'm sure we can. Okay?'

'Okay Grandad,' Jack managed in between his sobs.

After breakfast Jack went up to bed. He took the tartan blanket from the bed, rolled it carefully and stowed it on top of the wardrobe before he got under the covers. He just wanted to sleep now, untroubled by dreams or other worlds or whatever they were. He felt guilty for shunning Willie in this way, but he just couldn't face anymore sadness that day. He lay there and thought of his mother and his new brother. He missed her so much. But if he was honest with himself, he had to admit that he wished his brother had never been born. And still Robert was his mum's son every bit as much as he was. He couldn't deny that. He was grateful when sleep finally came.

When Jack heard the front door opening he woke with a start. It felt like he had been sleeping for days rather than hours. He went to the window and looked out at the street. It was bright still, but cloudy; probably only mid-afternoon. He put on his jeans and a sweatshirt and found some clean socks and pulled on his trainers.

He heard footsteps on the stairs and for a moment he feared that Robert had come back and that Grandad was going to insist that they talk. He stood by his bed and waited for the door to open.

'Jack, you're a lazy so and so!' Peadar cried as he barged into the room.

'Peadar, it's you!' Jack said, relieved.

'Why, were you expecting somebody else?'

Jack shook his head and laughed.

'No,' he said. 'Hey, come here and look at this.' Jack took the tartan blanket from the top of the wardrobe.

'It's a blanket – so what?' Peadar said, disappointed.

'Not just any blanket,' Jack said. 'It belonged to my grandmother.'

'We have blankets like that at home too,' Peadar said.

'Not like this one, you don't.' Jack smiled at his friend.

'So what's so special about it?' Peadar asked, reaching out and touching the corner of it.

'It's magic Peadar.'

'No way! I like magic in books, but this is the real world.'

'It *is* magic. When I sleep with this blanket around me I go back to 1916. But when I fold it up and put it away I just sleep.'

'So you're saying that this blanket is a kind of time portal?' Peadar asked, looking interested.

'A time portal, yeah, that's a good name for it Peadar. I don't know why or how it works, but it really does take me back.'

'So that means that if I sleep wrapped up in it then I'll go back to 1916 too?'

'I suppose so.' Jack looked concerned.

'We should really test it then, shouldn't we? Just to be scientific about it.'

'What do you mean?' Jack asked.

'I should take it home with me tonight and try it out. If I go back to 1916 then it really is a portal. If I don't, then maybe this whole thing is just down to you, and your – you know – imagination.'

'But I showed you the manifesto – I've already proved that it's real.'

'That's true. But to be really scientific we must prove beyond any doubt that this blanket has special properties. Let's give it a go, Jack!'

Peadar reached across and took the blanket in his arms. He held it up to his face and scrutinised the fabric, picking at it with his fingertips.

'It looks like any other blanket to me,' he said.

Jack grabbed the blanket roughly from Peadar's hands.

'You're not taking it anywhere Peadar. I need it here. Tonight I have to go back to make sure Willie and his family are alright. They live near the GPO and the shelling has started already.'

Peadar looked disappointed. He walked over to the window and looked out.

'Oh God! There's that fella Paddy Barton outside on his bike,' Peadar said.

Jack stood beside him at the window. He looked down and saw Biker free wheeling down the street past the house. When he got a little way past he turned and cycled back around again.

'I don't care about him,' Jack said.

'I don't like the way he keeps showing up Jack. It's not good,' Peadar said. 'He got expelled from my school for setting fire to a cloakroom, you know.'

Barton cycled off then, back the way he'd come, towards the South Circular Road. Peadar turned back to Jack.

'I'd love to see what it's like in 1916,' he said. 'Can I not go with you?'

'No, I don't think so. I mean, how could you?'

'I could have a sleepover with you. I could ask my Mam – I'm sure she wouldn't mind.'

'Tonight?'

'Yeah, why not? You say it to your grandad now and I'll go home and see if Mam will let me.'

'I'm not sure Peadar.' Jack was wondering about Willie. What would he say when Jack showed up with another boy?

'Come on!' Peadar was excited now. 'Please Jack! I can help you with Willie and his family.'

Within minutes Jack found himself downstairs with Peadar easily convincing Grandad that Peadar sleeping over that night would be a good idea. When Peadar ran off home to pack a few things and get permission from his mother Jack grew more and more uneasy at the prospect of bringing his two friends together.

That evening he and Peadar played cards with Grandad at the kitchen table until it was late enough to allow them to go upstairs to bed.

'Now how does this work?' Peadar asked when they got into the bedroom.

'Well, we need to sleep and the blanket needs to be across the two of us I think for it to work.'

'Oh God, I don't know how I'm going to sleep with all the excitement,' Peadar said.

At first they tried sleeping head to toe, but that didn't work. Peadar's feet smelled and Jack could feel a draught every time Peadar moved in the bed. Finally they lay down side by side, listening to the noises from the street outside; the occasional car or idle chat or burst of laughter from passers-by. Jack's eyes were wide open, staring at the grey ceiling that was tinged with an orange glow from the streetlight outside his bedroom window. He listened to Peadar's even breathing.

He thought he would never sleep, so he was surprised when Peadar's voice woke him suddenly.

'Are you asleep yet Jack?'

'I was.'

'Sorry. I slept for a bit, but I didn't dream at all. Maybe the blanket won't work for me.'

'Don't think about it Peadar. Just sleep now.'

Jack felt so tired. All he wanted to do was to close his eyes and let sleep overtake him. It was like giving up or giving in to something, he thought. Sometimes he wished he could just stop everything; stop time, stop growing, stop life, stop changing. Changing was the hardest thing. Him changing. Other people changing. Not being able to go back, just forward all the time even if the future was uncertain. Only in the past was there any certainty.

'Do you want to play football on my team Jack?' Peadar asked.

'What team?'

'My Gaelic football team,' he said.

'Sure, okay. I'd like to try it.'

'I think you'd be good. You have a great kick on you and you're tough.'

'Okay, but be quiet now. Let's sleep.'

Chapter 17

All around him there was banging and clanging. Further off the thumping of heavy artillery could be heard, and further again the pockety-pock of machine gun fire. He was lying among a pile of rags, a kind of makeshift bed, in a laneway off the quays. He could hear the slapping of the river against the quay wall, as regular as a heart-beat. His whole body ached from lying on the hard cobbles. He shivered. It was the fall of evening and the lights should have been going on along the street, but they did not. And yet there was a lightening in the sky above the buildings as if it was dawn and not dusk. Jack knew where he was and who he was, and then he remembered Peadar. He got up and wandered up and down the lane calling his friend's name quietly.

When he was satisfied that Peadar was not around he headed out onto the quays and walked towards the bridge. No museum exhibit or any amount of old photographs in books could have prepared him for the sight that met his eyes when he turned left onto Sackville Street. Half of the buildings were demolished altogether; the Metropole Hotel, which he had walked past only two nights ago, was razed to the ground. Clerys department store was hardly more than a shell, but up ahead the GPO appeared to stand much as it was. Fires burned in the wreckage of buildings and women and children scavenged among the debris of shops, retrieving anything of value they could find, careless of the shells that continued to whistle overhead en route from the river.

He was worried about Peadar and where he might be, but he was not frightened for himself. As he walked on he was appalled by the destruction he saw all around him. He remembered how beautiful the street had been in the spring sunshine only days before and he was saddened. But then he thought of all the families who lived nearby, all the homes that must have been destroyed or abandoned or both. No wonder they searched among the debris for something of value. These people had nothing and their children had nothing.

As he neared the GPO, the shelling stopped for a while and he ran past the front of the building as fast as he could and around to Henry Street, eager to see if Willie's house remained unscathed. It was only when he stepped onto Henry Street that he saw the true state of the Rising's Headquarters. The building he thought to be largely undamaged from the front was just that; a mere façade behind which there was little of substance. The roof and the side walls were almost completely destroyed, and Jack could clearly see the extent of the suffering inflicted on the volunteers inside. He was reminded of a documentary he'd seen at school on the lives of bees, where one wall of the hive was made of glass to allow the beekeepers and the cameras to show clearly the day to day comings and goings of the queen and the drones.

Jack searched among the tattered battalion for Seán, but he could not find him. He asked one or two of the men, but they did not answer him. All of the spirit and optimism of days before had fled and was replaced by a heavy gloom brought on by the imminent taste of defeat and failure which stuck in their throats.

He felt like a ghost moving among the ruins of buildings and men until a young nurse from Cumann na mBan asked him who he was.

'My name is Jack,' he replied. 'I'm looking for Seán Mahon – his brother, Willie, is my friend.'

'I don't know Seán,' she said. 'Was he fighting here?'

'Yes, under Pearse and Connolly – we came to see him a couple of days ago.'

'A lot has changed since then,' she said. 'He may be wounded and if so he might be in the Richmond or Jervis Street Hospital. They will look after him there. You should go home. It's too dangerous to be abroad now.'

'But I have to find my friend, Willie.'

Just then the shelling started again. Plaster and stonework began to crumble and fall around them.

'Just go on now young fella. You can't be out here anymore.'

'If you see Seán, tell him I will look after Willie and not to be worried.'

'I will. Now go on home. The next time the shells stop falling there'll be soldiers outside breaking in, shooting anything that moves. It's only a matter of time.'

As he left, Jack noticed Connolly lying on an improvised stretcher made from an old wooden door. Blood seeped from wounds on his arm and his ankle, but he smiled at Jack nonetheless and winked at him.

'We're still here, wee man, we're still here,' he said.

Back out on Henry Street night had fallen completely and Jack ran from the bombs in the direction of Cuckoo Lane where Willie's family were now living. He looked back as he ran and it seemed as though the whole city was on fire.

Cuckoo Lane was a terrace of tenements and, while Jack had seen which door Willie's mother had entered by, he had no idea where to go when inside. He did not relish the prospect of tramping through the squalid lives of the poor of Dublin. The dank staircase that opened up to him at the doorway was not inviting, so he simply stood outside and waited for a while.

He could hear gunfire nearby, to the north, and he found himself drawn to it despite the danger. He wandered up the dark street onto North King Street where he was almost run over by a huge armoured truck. Soldiers ran in its wake, heads bent low, with rifles clutched in their hands. He slunk back down the lane off the main thoroughfare and listened as more shots were exchanged. Volleys of rounds were fired from the belly of the armoured vehicle by soldiers hidden inside. It was too dangerous to be out, he decided. There must have been a volunteer stronghold somewhere nearby and the soldiers, tired and on edge, would shoot at anything that moved.

The night had grown chilly and a fine mist of rain now fell. He walked back past the Tenements on Cuckoo Lane and on down to the quays. Throughout it all he could hear the shells continuing to fall on Sackville Street, and crossing over Kings Bridge he heard more gunfire coming to meet him. It was coming from the south, the direction in which he was headed. He didn't meet another soul as he walked towards the South Circular Road, but the shots were closer now. The street lights here had failed to light too and he found himself tripping on the cobbles or over rubbish that had been wheeled out into the street to make up barricades. He had no idea how near or far he was from home and he wished more than anything that he could be back in his room asleep, dry and warm and safe.

It bothered him that Willie had not shown up. He hoped that he was safe, but feared the worst. And worse again was the feeling in his stomach when he remembered their last exchange. He thought of Peadar then. He wished that Peadar was here with him to share in the sadness he felt. But Peadar could never know the extent of his hopelessness – nobody could. He wondered why the blanket only worked for him. It was like fate maybe. This unique upheaval was Jack's and Jack's alone to witness.

He was soaked right through and cold, so cold. He doubted he would ever find Grandad's house without a light to guide him. He stumbled on as best he could, his hands stretched out in front of him, his steps faltering like those of a blind man. With a sudden thump he smacked his shin on the discarded frame of an old upturned pram. The pain was unbearable. He sat down on the wet road rubbing his leg while hot tears sprung from his eyes. It wasn't fair. He was giving up, giving in to tears that had been building up inside him for days. He had never wanted to come here. He only ever wanted to be happy, to be allowed to be the ordinary boy he was, the boy who tried his best at school, who enjoyed football and television and computer games. Until he came to Dublin that was who he was. Now he was someone else; he was Irish, he had a Grandad who spent his life thinking about the past, he had a brother he never knew about, and he had a history that was full of sadness. He looked up into the darkness, the rain and the tears on his face became indistinguishable, and he shouted out with all his might:

'I'm English for God's sake! English! Do you hear me?'

He wasn't sure who he was shouting at, but he got a reply.

'That's funny, you told me you were Irish.'

Willie was standing over him, smiling with a lantern in his hand and his mother's tartan blanket draped around his shoulders.

'I was looking for you all over the place,' he said.

Jack couldn't speak. He was crying a little, but smiling at the same time. Willie helped him to his feet.

'Have you hurt yourself Jack?' he asked, holding the light down to Jack's knee.

Jack rolled up his pyjama leg and wiped the blood from a gash on his shin with his palm.

'I'm okay,' he said. 'I couldn't see a thing. All the streetlights are out. I was trying to get back to Grandad's.'

'I've just come from that way. It's much too dangerous. Do you hear all the gunfire? That's from the Union – they've been going at it hammer and tongs these past hours. You better come on home with me.'

'But your aunt, will she mind?'

'She won't mind. She found room for us and she'll find room for you too.'

Jack followed Willie back up towards Kingsbridge station. He felt better now that his friend was there again. Willie gave him the blanket and Jack wrapped himself up in it to keep out the cold as they walked. As they crossed over the bridge they could see the sky over Sackville Street lit up like a firework display. Jack wanted to ask Willie about Seán but didn't have the heart to tell him that he wasn't at the GPO when he looked for him earlier.

'It's not going well, is it Willie?' It was more of a statement than a question.

'No, Jack, it's not. We thought the rest of the country would have risen up by now, but it hasn't happened. The city's full of soldiers too.'

'What will they do?' Jack asked, even though he knew the answer.

'They'll fight on, that's what they'll do.'

'But it won't do any good. More people will die or be wounded, more houses will be destroyed.'

Willie stopped in his tracks and looked Jack in the eye.

'I said the very same thing to Seán the other day and do you know what he said to me?'

Willie's eyes shone in the yellow light of the lantern.

'He said: "The eyes of the world are on us now Willie and we must show them our desire for freedom."'

With that he turned and walked on ahead towards the tenements. Safe inside, among the heat of many other bodies, Jack made his bed on the floor beside his friend. He wrapped himself in the blanket Willie had given him and closed his eyes. Sleep eluded him despite his tiredness and he listened to the distant rumblings of guns and the snores and coughs of his invisible bed fellows.

Chapter 18

'Jack! Jack! Wake up!'

'What? What is it?'

Jack was lying on the floor beside his bed wrapped in the tartan blanket. Peadar was kneeling beside him, peering into his face.

'You were making some awful noises,' he said. 'Did you dream then?'

Jack nodded. He felt exhausted.

'And you?' he asked.

Peadar shook his head, disappointed.

'I never slept so well in my life,' he said. 'Not even the whiff of a dream.'

'So what does that mean, scientifically speaking?' Jack asked.

'I'm not sure,' Peadar said, as he stood up. 'It could have something to do with the fact that you pulled the blanket off me during the night. Did the dream feel real again this time?'

'It's not a dream Peadar. Every time it's more real than the last. It's real Peadar, I know it is.'

'And your friend, Willie, is he okay?' Peadar asked.

'Yes, but I'm worried about his brother, Seán. I was at the GPO and the place was in ruins, but there was no sign of him. I spoke to a nurse there, but she didn't even know who he was.'

'It doesn't mean he isn't okay,' Peadar said.

'I know. I saw Connolly too, he didn't look well. He was wounded. He spoke to me, Peadar.'

'That's weird, Jack – you're freaking me out,' Peadar said shaking his head.

'I know, nothing surprises me anymore,' Jack said as he got to his feet and peeled the blanket from himself.

'I can imagine.'

'No you can't, Peadar. It's not just 1916. There's more.'

Jack had wanted to talk to somebody since he found out about Robert being his brother, but he found it hard to talk to Grandad about it. Jack could tell that Robert's arrival had upset him too, brought him back to less happier times that he had no wish to revisit.

'You know that guy who was hanging around? Robert Burke is his name.'

'You mean the fella that stopped us on the street the other day?'

Jack nodded.

'Yeah, what about him?'

'It turns out he's my stepbrother,' Jack said as evenly as he could.

'What?'

'My mother had him years ago before she moved to London and he was adopted. He contacted her earlier in the year and they've been writing to each other. When she stopped answering his letters a few weeks back he panicked and came looking for Grandad.'

'God Jack! I don't know what to say.' Peadar's mouth remained open for some time after he spoke.

'Me neither. That's how he knew my name when he tried to stop us on the street that time. I understand that we're brothers Peadar, but I'm not sure that I really want a brother. I don't want to meet him, not right now. Is that wrong?'

'No, it's not wrong. If your mam was here now this wouldn't be happening. She wouldn't want you to be upset.'

'I know. But everything makes me upset these days. Everything is so… different.'

Jack sat down on the bed and dropped his head. He looked worn out, defeated. Peadar looked around the room as if he was looking for something that might distract Jack from his dark mood.

'You said you'd come to football training with me this afternoon. You'll love it and it'll take your mind off Willie and Seán, and Robert too – for a while anyway.'

'I don't know Peadar. Gaelic football, I mean, it's not really me.'

Peadar sat down beside him on the edge of the bed.

'Come on, I've seen you play soccer, you're really good, and you've seen the Dubs in action so you know what it's all about.'

Peadar smiled at him. Jack found it hard to say no to someone who was always so positive.

'Okay then, I suppose,' he said, and almost immediately he felt a little better, a little stronger. 'But there's one thing I want you to do for me before we go.'

'No problem Jack. Just tell me and it's done.'

'You've got a computer at your place, haven't you?'

'Of course – it's Sally's, but she won't mind.'

'Good we'll go over to yours after breakfast.'

Jack wouldn't tell Peadar what he wanted to check until they were safe inside Peadar's room with Sally's laptop open on the bed.

'I want you to Google the children who died in the Rising. I need to know that Willie will be okay. The days are passing and the city is being blown to pieces. I just need to know that he's going to be okay.'

'Are you sure?' Peadar asked.

'I'm sure. I have to know.'

While Peadar was busy tapping at the keys Jack couldn't bear to even look over his friend's shoulder. He waited, and he thought that his whole life had become a form of waiting; waiting for his life to return to normal, waiting to hear some good news about his mother.

'I'm looking through the list now. What did you say his surname was?'

'Mahon. Willie Mahon,' Jack said, and as he said it he could almost see the name as it must surely appear on the screen in front of Peadar. More waiting.

Peadar was no longer tapping the keys, but he wasn't speaking either. Jack realised how strange it was to be in a room with Peadar and for him to be silent.

'What is it Peadar? Have you found him?'

'I don't know.'

'Either his name is there or it isn't,' Jack said, for the first time looking over his friend's shoulder at the screen.

'There is a William Mahon, but it might not be him.' Peadar tried to close the laptop but Jack reached out a hand and stopped him.

'It's him alright. Age twelve. Oh God Peadar, I wish I never asked you to look!'

'I'm sorry,' Peadar said.

'It's not your fault.'

Jack turned away from his friend and was quiet. He did not want Peadar to see him crying. He felt trapped by every circumstance of his life. Willie's death was already a fact, so how could he alter that? But there had to be something he could do. Crying was no good to anyone now. He managed to control himself before he turned back to Peadar, but he sensed that there would be plenty more tears shed in the future.

'I shouldn't have looked that up for you Jack,' Peadar said. 'I'm sorry.'

'No, no, don't be silly Peadar. I would have found out anyway.'

Jack was quiet for a while.

'So what are you going to do about it, Jack?'

'I'm not sure yet.'

'You're not going to go back there again, are you?'

Peadar looked at him with wide open eyes, his head to one side.

'You can't, Jack. Just put the blanket away forever and forget all about it.'

'But I can't, Peadar. I can't just abandon him, knowing what I know now.'

The pitch where the team trained was muddy and not very flat, but it didn't seem to matter to anyone. About twenty boys of Jack's age showed up and Peadar proudly introduced Jack as a friend of his from London. Jack was wearing old tracksuit bottoms and his best Arsenal top and was surprised to find that the colours of other Premier League teams featured along with the blue of Dublin. Two cross looking men called Colm and Frank were the trainers and Jack was beginning to regret agreeing to come along when one of them approached him.

'Have you ever played football before?' Colm asked.

'Oh yes, I play for my school in London,' Jack said.

'We're talking about real football now Jack,' Frank interjected, 'not that namby-pamby game you play over there.'

Colm winked at him.

'No,' Jack said, 'I've never played Gaelic Football before, but I went to see the Dubs last Sunday.'

'No worries so,' Colm said, 'you'll be flying in no time. Just watch what the other lads are doing.'

Frank handed out blue and red bibs and they split into two groups to do training drills.

'Because Jack is here today we're going to go back to basics,' Frank said.

There was a general groan from the boys. Some of them were chatting and pushing each other and Frank let out such a loud roar at them that Jack's heart jumped in his chest.

'Don't mind Frank,' Peadar whispered to him, 'his bark is worse than his bite. Just stick with me, okay?'

Jack nodded.

The first drill was peculiar. Two lines of boys faced each other and the ball was on the ground in the middle. Jack watched closely as the first boy ran to the ball, bent over and lifted the ball from his toe into his hand. Frank shouted instructions over the general racket the boys made as they got ready to lift.

'Get yer toe under it! You can't touch the ball on the ground or it's a free against you on match day!'

Jack's turn came and he ran to the ball as quickly as he could. He concentrated hard, remembering the way the other boys had done it. He bent over and stretched out his hands to gather the ball, but he kicked it too hard and it flew through his hands and across the field.

'Go and get that ball!' Frank yelled.

Jack reddened and went to retrieve it. Colm came over to him then and smiled at him.

'No one does it right first time Jack, don't be worried. Here let me have the ball.'

Jack gave him the ball and watched as Colm bent over slowly and performed the pick up a few times in a row.

'Do you see now? It's easy. Just keep your fingers spread with the thumbs almost touching. Now you try it.'

Colm dropped the ball on the grass and Jack bent over, his brow furrowed in concentration, and performed a clean lift.

'There you are,' he said. 'Now go on back in the line and show them how it's done.'

Peadar smiled at him as he took his place in the line again and this time he lifted the ball cleanly and quickly first time.

'Great pick up, Jack!' Frank shouted.

The next drill was harder. The boys had to solo the ball in two groups and pass the ball back and forth using their fists. Peadar showed Jack how to use the hard part at the heel of the hand to give more power to the pass, but he hadn't a clue how to solo. At first he just kicked the ball away every time, and when Colm told him to turn his toe upwards he kicked the ball over his own head. He began to get frustrated with himself and he could hear some of the other boys laughing among themselves each time he failed. The boy he was paired with, Martin, started complaining to Frank.

'Can I not swap partner Frank? This is crazy – he just keeps kicking the ball away!'

Frank ignored him, but every time Jack fluffed a solo he could hear Martin sighing and swearing under his breath. He couldn't get Willie out of his head; he kept seeing his face every time he shut his eyes to catch his breath. He was fed up with Martin's sarcastic remarks and had just decided to run off home when Colm blew his whistle and called all the boys together. They were going to have a practice match, blues versus reds. This was better, he thought. He was on the blue team with Peadar, but unfortunately so was Martin.

Frank and Colm picked positions for all the boys and there were a lot of complaints and arguments from most of the boys who wanted to be in mid-field. Jack was happy to be picked as a forward because that was his position when he played soccer. Peadar came over to him briefly before the game started to give him some advice.

'If you get the ball just have a shot, but if you're crowded out try and use a fist pass to me or one of the other lads. Oh and don't mind anything that Martin says – he's a good player but he's a bit of a mouth.'

When the game started, Jack could see straight away that Martin and Peadar were the two strongest players on the blue team. Jack struggled to remember all the boys' names, but when he could remember a name he called for the ball and made runs into space. No one was passing to him however, except for Peadar. At one point Peadar was clean through for a shot on goal but he passed it to Jack. Jack fumbled the ball and the defender was able to clear it away.

'You have to take your chances Peadar!' Martin shouted at him. 'That eejit is just going to waste every ball you give him!'

Jack was furious, but he said nothing. Peadar smiled at him and threw his eyes up to heaven.

A few minutes later Martin came bursting through with the ball, but there were three boys around him preventing him from getting a shot in. Jack ran towards him calling for the ball, shouting Martin's name at the top of his voice, but the pass never came. Colm blew his whistle for a free.

'Free against you Martin, travelling. You've got to use it or lose it!' he said.

'Why didn't you pass to me?' Jack asked Martin.

'Leave me alone!' Martin said as he ran back up the pitch.

Jack followed him.

'You just had to pass it, I was right there!' he said.

Martin's face was red and he turned to Jack and pushed him away.

'Stop annoying me, ya sap! Why would I give the ball to you? I might as well give it away to the reds!'

Jack came right back at him and pushed Martin hard. People didn't generally fight back when Martin started on them so he was momentarily surprised to find himself being shoved around.

He smiled at Jack then, a sinister smile.

'Why don't you just go home? We don't want you here. Go back to England, or maybe you don't have a home!'

In that moment while Martin was talking, while he was still slightly off balance from the push, Jack made up his mind to let him have it. He pulled back his closed fist and punched Martin hard on the side of the head. Martin fell. No one expected that. He fell to his knees first and then forward onto his face and into the mud.

The whistle shrieked and boys from both teams gathered around Jack, some trying to fight with him, others defending him. Peadar grabbed his arm and led him away as quickly as he could. While Colm helped Martin to his feet, Frank stormed over to where Peadar and Jack were standing. He pointed at Jack, his face a mask of anger.

'You!' he said. 'You can't do that! Do you hear me?'

Jack nodded. He felt weak, ill, as if he might get sick.

'I'm sorry,' he said, but he wasn't sorry. He was thinking about Willie and what was about to happen to him. He fought back the tears again.

Frank looked at Peadar.

'Peadar you'll have to take him home. He can't come back, do you hear me? We can't have this kind of carry on.'

Peadar nodded.

'I'm sorry Frank, I don't know what came over me,' Jack said.

'Listen, I know you're not a bad kid, and I know Martin can bring out the worst in all of us at times. But fighting, I just can't have it. Now go on home before there's any more trouble, okay?'

Home. That was just it. Jack didn't know where home was anymore. By the time the boys set off the match had re-started. As they left the pitch they could see Martin sitting on the far sideline cradling his head in his hands.

'That was some knockout punch!' Peadar said. 'Did you ever consider taking up boxing?'

'No,' Jack replied, 'not until now.'

They looked at each other and burst out laughing.

'You know, I never hit anyone ever before in my life,' Jack said.

The boys walked on in silence for a while until Jack spoke again.

'I hope I haven't caused trouble for you at the club because of this,' he said.

'No, don't be silly. It wasn't your fault, even Frank could see that. But you picked the wrong fella to hit.'

'What do you mean?'

'Martin. Martin Kelly. He's Trevor Kelly's younger brother.'

For a moment Jack couldn't place the name. Then his heart sank. Ugly. The boy who'd tried to rob him on his second day.

'Oh God, I don't believe it Peadar.'

They walked on in silence for a while.

'Apart from all that, how did you enjoy your first taste of Gaelic football?' Peadar asked.

'It was alright,' Jack said, 'but I think I'll stick with soccer. It's safer I reckon.'

Chapter 19

Grandad was making the tea when Jack got home; there were rashers on the grill and he was cutting a fresh loaf of bread into thick slices which he smothered with real salty butter. Jack's heart sank. This level of excess only signalled one thing: a visitor was coming, and Jack had a good idea who it might be.

'Enjoy the football then?' Grandad asked as he filled the large teapot with boiling water.

'Yeah, it was good.' Jack had decided he would not tell Grandad about the incident with Martin.

'So you'll be joining the team then,' he said. It wasn't really a question, so Jack decided it didn't warrant a response. He sat at the table.

'So who's coming for tea?' Jack asked.

Grandad stopped what he was doing and looked at his grandson.

'Who said anyone was coming for tea?'

'Well, you're cooking bacon for starters, and there's no sign of the usual boiled eggs,' Jack said.

'Aren't you the smart alec?' Grandad smiled. 'There's no hiding things from you; you're your mother's son alright.' He shook his head and laughed quietly to himself.

'Is it Robert?' Jack asked.

'It is,' Grandad replied. He paused for a moment. 'I feel sorry for him, to be honest. He's come looking for his mother and in the process he's fallen out with his adoptive family.' His eyes pleaded, but Jack just looked at him blankly. 'If you must know I feel guilty, for the way I behaved when he was born.'

There was a sharp sliver of annoyance in his voice and Jack heard it, but he didn't blame Grandad for it. No, he blamed Robert. Grandad sighed loudly, a long slow exhalation, as if he had been holding his breath for hours.

'It's awkward I know. We're all family, but we don't know each other yet. Whatever way I look at it, I think I owe him something. You're innocent in all this, Jack. I'm sorry you got dragged into the middle of it. If your mother was here she would have handled it all much better than me. I was taken by surprise; I wasn't ready for Robert when he came calling.'

Jack wished Grandad would stop talking. He didn't blame him for anything; he'd been more than good to Jack since he arrived. Grandads were supposed to be cheerful and wise, not worried and guilty, and Jack resented Robert all the more because of the way he was making Grandad feel. There was nothing Grandad could say that would help matters or change things in any tangible way so Jack wished he would just stop trying and stop being so hard on himself.

The doorbell rang and both of them froze for a moment. Jack's stomach turned over and he thought that he might be sick. As he went to the door Grandad whispered to him.

'Don't worry lad. Just go wash your hands. Everything will be grand, you'll see.'

Jack scurried out into the hall and upstairs to the loo before Grandad could open the door. He stood at the top of the stairs for a moment and listened.

'Ah Robert, there you are,' Grandad said.

'Hello Mick, thanks for inviting me.'

'Not at all, come on in. The tea is nearly ready.'

They moved into the living room. Jack leaned over the banister and strained to listen to their conversation.

'Is Jack around?' Robert asked.

'Yes, he'll be down in a minute. He's just back from football training.'

Jack's heart sank. Why did Robert want to see him? What did he want from him? Jack couldn't care less if he saw his mother or his grandfather, but why the hell should he be dragged into it too? Robert was a stranger, nothing more or less. He was twenty-three years old for goodness sake! Why would he want to be friends with a twelve year old? He wished he'd gone over to Peadar's for tea.

He went into the bathroom and washed his hands. He dried them slowly with the hand towel and then stood there in front of the wash hand basin, staring at his reflection in the mirror. It had always just been him and his mother. And then in the last two years Matt came along, but that was okay. He was really only an extra. Jack was still first when it came to his mother's affections. Grandad was calling him. He could hear him clearly above the noise of the radio and the kettle coming to boil. He trudged down the stairs slowly as if in a dream. But this was real and he knew it.

'Ah there he is now!' Grandad declared. 'Robert is here to see us Jack.'

Robert stood up. Even to Jack it seemed an awkward, formal gesture.

'Hi Jack, it's good to see you again.' He smiled at Jack and sat down.

Jack sat at the table between Robert and Grandad. The tea had already been poured and each plate contained two rashers, a quartered tomato and a hunk of buttered white loaf bread.

'Now,' Grandad said as he began to eat.

Jack waited for him to say something more, but he didn't, so they ate in silence for five minutes until Grandad got up to refill the mugs of tea. The silence was unbearable.

'How long have you lived here?' Robert asked Grandad.

Jack could see that Grandad was nervous.

'Oh we've always been here, since just after I got married – 1960 I think.'

'So my mother,' Robert looked at Jack for a second, 'so Kate would have grown up in this house?'

'Yes. Where Jack sleeps now, that was her room for years, until... until... well, that was her room.'

'I see yes,' Robert said and he looked down at his plate.

There was a momentary silence which Grandad did his best to fill.

'And you, Robert, where did you grow up?' he asked.

'We lived in Cork, just outside Carrigaline when I was small. But my dad got a job in Cork City when I was a teenager so we moved nearer the city then. I didn't like that as much.'

'And do you have brothers and sisters?' Grandad asked.

Jack looked from one to the other as they talked and he felt as if he was a ghost, invisible to them.

'Yes, I have a sister, Maura, she's a few years younger than me.'
'Oh well, that's nice,' Grandad said.
'Well, no, we don't really get along very well. Not anymore.'
'No? Why is that?' Grandad was being ever so polite, showing such an interest in Robert and eating only small mouthfuls at a time and actually using his knife and fork.

'When I turned eighteen my mother – my adoptive mother – explained to me who I was and since then I've been interested in finding my birth parents. Maura thinks I should just leave things alone; she says that I'm upsetting Mam by pursuing it. I tried to leave it for a while, but it's important to me. She should understand that, but she doesn't. I'm sure Mam understands.'

'I'm sure she does Robert, but for people of my generation it can be difficult to accept.' Grandad was being tactful, probably mindful also of his own part in Robert's story.

'So are you working in Dublin?' Grandad asked quickly.

'Not yet. I'm looking, but there's not much out there.'

'I'm sure you'll get something soon – a bright young fella like you,' Grandad said.

Jack wondered why Grandad was being so unlike himself.

'I finished college last year in Cork,' Robert went on. 'I promised myself when I got my degree I would find my real mother.'

'I see,' Grandad said slowly. 'What did you study there?'

'Arts,' Robert replied.

'Do you hear that Jack, Arts – isn't that something?'

Grandad looked at him, but Jack simply shrugged his shoulders and swallowed another mouthful of bread.

'I wanted to be sure to get my degree first,' Robert said. 'I knew people would blame me and my search for my mother if I failed my exams. So I waited.'

'Very wise,' Grandad nodded.

The silence threatened them again and Grandad acted swiftly to keep it at bay.

'And your family – in Cork – they're all well?' he asked.

'Yes, well my father died a few years back. He had a stroke. So it's just me and my mother and sister now.'

'Oh, I'm sorry,' Grandad said. 'But it's important to look after them and not upset them too much.'

'I never set out to upset anyone!' Robert raised his voice momentarily and checked himself quickly.

'God knows I know that Robert,' Grandad soothed. 'It's just people of my generation are slow to accept change, you know?'

'It's not just your generation, Mick,' Robert said. 'My sister's the worst – practically accuses me of breaking my mother's heart!'

'I'm sure she doesn't mean it really. She's probably just worried about her mother and about you too.'

'Yeah, maybe. But there's others too,' he said, and he nodded his head in Jack's direction.

'Ah now, he's only a child. He has nothing to do with any of this,' Grandad said.

'But he's my brother, flesh and blood, not like Maura,' Robert said.

Jack was almost convinced now that he was actually invisible. The way they talked about him as if he was not there.

Jack stood up quickly from the table, making himself visible again.

'I may be your brother, but it doesn't mean I have to like you,' he declared, and with that he ran out of the room and upstairs to his room. He wrapped himself in his grandmother's tartan blanket and lay on the bed. He could hear muffled noises from below, formless words being exchanged, the clink and clatter of cups and plates, water running. He did the thing he always tried not to do; he began to think of his mother and how things were before she left him here, before she got sick. He thought about school then and football matches at the Emirates stadium and he thought about London and how much better it was than Dublin. He wished, not for the first time, that he had never set foot in this place.

Outside on the street there was a scurry of boots and a crash of broken glass. He thought he heard laughter. He got up and went to the window. With the bedroom light off he was able to see the street below clearly. Nothing stirred. He was fairly sure he'd heard something so he stood by the window for some time until he was satisfied no one was there.

He got back into bed. He could still hear them talking downstairs. He hadn't meant to be so rude to Robert, but he made it seem as if he, Jack, was somehow the cause of Robert being adopted. Jack knew that was impossible, but he felt as if he *was* responsible every time Robert looked at him or spoke to him. But he shouldn't have shouted at Robert, he knew that. When he thought about it he actually felt sorry for him. Grandad was right. To find out at eighteen that the people you thought were your Mum and Dad were not must have been awful. It was no wonder he was a bit odd sometimes; it was as if he was consumed by that knowledge and hell bent on finding his real parents no matter what he had to do. And now he'd finally found his birth mother.

It was thinking about what would happen next that bothered Jack most. That dreaded phrase: the future. That was the thing that frightened him most. All through his short life he was confident of what each new day would bring before it came. His mother had always made him feel secure. Now it was different. Every day now, and even every night when he lay in bed and closed his eyes, almost anything could happen and that's what frightened him.

There were more noises from outside again; laughter and a thumping sound, as if someone was hammering in the distance. He went to the window again and looked out at the twilit street. The streetlights had come on since he'd last looked out, but the street seemed as quiet as ever. He waited and waited until he saw Biker emerge from a laneway on the far side of the road. He turned and raised a hand and four other figures followed him into the street. The one at the rear was familiar – Trevor Kelly, his blond shaven head, his face scarred red with acne. There could be no mistake.

He thought about going down to tell Grandad, but what would he say. Perhaps they were just passing by and if Grandad went out to them it would only identify his house for them and they might make his life a misery. The fact that Robert was there still helped him make up his mind to stay put also. If he went down he would certainly have to apologise for his earlier rude behaviour and he was not ready just yet to do that.

He pulled the curtains and lay back down on the bed. He wrapped himself up in his grandmother's tartan blanket and closed his eyes. He had often felt sorry for himself before, but never like this. He wanted only to sleep, to forget everything.

When he woke it was pitch dark. He could see the orange glow of the streetlight outside his curtained window. He listened and he thought he heard a hissing noise that reminded him of the sound of the sea when he lay down on a towel on the beach during the summer and shut his eyes. There was a peculiar smell in the air also and his sleepy mind tried to rouse itself to name it. Fireworks on bonfire night, he decided finally, and for a moment he had to remind himself that he was in Grandad's house in Dublin and that it was spring, not autumn.

He got up and went out onto the landing. It was brighter out here, glowing orange like the street lights outside, and the smell was stronger. So strong, in fact, that he could almost see it as a kind of haze before his heavy eyes. Leaning across the banisters he was horrified to see the hall ablaze with black smoke rising up around the walls. He tried to scream but his voice did not project. He ran into his Grandad's room, but the bed was empty and still made up. He went back to his room and took the tartan blanket from the bed and, holding it around his head, he tried to make his way downstairs, but the heat and the smoke made it impossible to get beyond the fourth step down.

He found his voice and screamed and screamed until the smoke was just too much for him. He crawled back up onto the landing, coughing and choking as he went. He lay on the carpet wrapped in the blanket and gave in to the fumes.

Chapter 20

He could smell smoke. He looked up and saw smoke wreathed around the lone figure of Nelson on his pillar. All around him there was terrible destruction. He was standing in the street outside the Gresham Hotel which was now nothing more than a crumbling shell. Hot bullets blasted the road and the buildings, zinging on either side of him.

'Jack! Jack! Get out of there!' Willie called as he ran towards him in the shade of the buildings.

'Willie! You're okay?' Jack shouted. He was so relieved to see his friend again, and he vowed to himself that we would do everything he could to look after him, to make sure he would be safe.

'Of course I am, but you won't be if you don't get in off the road!'

He ran to Willie and together they made their way in the shelter of the buildings onto Great Britain Street and into relative safety.

'I was worried about you Willie,' Jack said.

'You don't have to worry about me! You'll get yourself killed, hanging around in the middle of the street like that, Jack.'

'Sorry, I was miles away. I was wondering how things will end for us.'

'It's not over yet,' Willie said. He did his best to smile.

'It's not good though, is it?' Jack asked.

'No, it's not. Even the leaders know it's only a matter of time.'

'So why don't they just stop now?'

'I don't know. Maybe they know something we don't, maybe there's still hope, maybe the Germans are on their way.'

'That's a lot of maybes,' Jack said.

The boys were heading towards the Four Courts. The fruit and vegetable markets, which were usually a hive of activity, were almost empty.

'Were you up at the GPO?' Jack asked.

'I was,' Willie said.

'And?'

'There's not much to report really.'

'And Seán, how is he?' Jack had to ask; he'd been on his mind since the last time he'd been to the GPO and he couldn't find him.

'He's okay. He took a bullet in the shoulder so they sent him to the hospital. All the Cumann na mBan women were sent away too – it's getting too dangerous – so there's no one there to dress the wounds except for one or two who refused to follow Pearse's direct command to leave.'

Jack was relieved. He was fairly sure that by the time Seán would be released the whole thing would be over. He hoped so anyway. But Willie – how could he protect him from the awful fact of history? He wracked his brains as they walked, but worryingly they seemed to be walking towards more trouble. The gunfire from North King Street was getting louder and was almost unbroken. The sound of engines revving could be heard above the ever-present cries of seagulls. Jack always found it hard to remember that Dublin was a city by the sea, and only the occasional appearance of these oversized, gluttonous birds served to remind him. They could appear anywhere; on the canal, in Grandad's back garden, in the heart of the city at all times of the day.

Willie wanted to check on his mother. She had very little food left at home and the shops were all closed still, so she was relying on the generosity of neighbours and friends to get by. Jack was appalled when he saw the state of their lodgings in daylight. The last time he'd been there it was night and he could only guess from the coughing and muttering the extent of the numbers that shared these shabby rooms. The smell was the worst thing, he thought. The dirt he could just about ignore, but the smell assaulted his nostrils no matter what he did or where he stood.

He pitied Willie and his family, particularly his mother, and he knew it was not right that they should leave her on her own with the children, but when Willie gave him the nod to go out to the street, he followed him immediately. Outside, even among the clamour of engines and gunfire, he could at least breathe.

'Where to now?' he asked.

'Let's head across the city and see if anything has changed at Jacobs or the Union.' Willie started walking and Jack trotted up beside him and kept pace.

Despite the warm sunshine the city had a peculiar air; the shops were all closed and there seemed to be soldiers everywhere. God knows how many had been shipped in from England during the course of the week.

'I meant to ask,' Willie said after a while, 'but how is your mother?'

Jack felt weird just thinking about her. When he was here with Willie his other life seemed so far away, almost unreal. But he had let it leak into this world the day he told Willie about his mother so he should have known that it would only be a matter of time before he asked about her.

'She's the same I think,' he said, trying to be as honest as he could with his friend. 'They don't tell me much, so I don't really know. They all say she'll be better soon, but I don't think I believe them.'

He had never admitted that much to himself before. As he said the words he acknowledged that this was actually how he felt; he feared the worst all the time, but kept it back inside himself. He was finding it harder and harder to be hopeful about the future. He was out of his depth and he knew it, like a tired swimmer battling vainly against the tide.

'I'm sorry Jack,' Willie said and he put his hand on Jack's shoulder as they walked on together. The weight of Willie's hand on his shoulder, coupled with the knowledge of his friend's dire fate, pressed down on Jack.

When they got near Jacobs there were soldiers everywhere in all the adjoining streets and they had built a cordon preventing anyone from passing anywhere near the building. The boys headed up towards the South Dublin Union following the sound of exchanged gunfire as they went. It was far too dangerous to be around there and even Willie agreed to leave without argument when Jack suggested they go home. Back in Cuckoo Lane Willie's mother gave them thin soup and bread to eat. Jack ate it hungrily, even though he would never have eaten soup at home for his mother. He was becoming accustomed to the way that Willie and his family lived. Only the smells continued to bother him; he was ashamed and wished he could be stronger. He watched Willie's mother feed and comfort her family with such tenderness it made him ache inside for his own mother.

As he sat there eating he made a hundred promises to himself about the way that he would be if only his mother would come back to him. He shut his eyes and wished and wished that she was there with him. He wished that Willie would be safe. He wasn't sure who granted wishes, but he wished all the same. Perhaps it was God. He wondered was he praying then. He didn't care if he was; he would gladly pray if he thought that it might make his wishes come true.

A small fire burned in the corner of the room and Willie's mother opened out a blanket and hung it on a line to heat for a while before she would wrap the smallest child in it to sleep. The blanket was exactly the same as the one in Grandad's house, the same one he'd wrapped himself up in when he slept there before. He noticed that there was a scorch mark on one corner that had not been there before. He reached and touched it, feeling the hard, blackened burn marks on the tips of his fingers. That would chafe at night against the child's soft skin if they were not careful.

'The blanket,' Jack said to Willie, 'it's been burned a bit.'

Willie seemed to be miles away, staring into the flames.

'Oh yeah? Must have been a spark from the fire,' he said absently.

Jack touched it again. It was familiar. He closed his eyes and the nobbled texture played on his fingers and on his mind bringing him somewhere else.

There was noise all around him. The rattle of implements, the clanking of trollies, doors banging, and many voices – some nearby, some distant – all carrying on indecipherable conversations. He opened his eyes again and shook his head quickly. The fireplace was gone, as was the blanket. And he was alone in a room and in bed, his hands clutching a hard woollen bedspread. He blinked a few times to adjust to the bright light. A curtain was pulled all around his bed. He tried to sit up and felt a sharp pinch in his right arm. A tube ran from his arm up to a drip. He found it hard to breathe, as if the room was starved of oxygen. The air was warm and heavy, dull with the smell of sickness and sterility. He settled back in the bed carefully and tried to imagine where he could be.

After a moment he remembered the fire. He had a vague memory of Robert bending down to lift him up. He did not remember how they escaped or if he'd been taken to hospital by ambulance – but he must have been. He must have passed out from all the smoke in the air. And Grandad? His heart missed a beat when he thought of the old man. A sour taste came into his mouth.

Outside the confined area around his bed he could hear movement and talking. He presumed there were other people in the ward with him and nurses going about their work, but when he tried to call out he found he had no voice. He was trapped until such time as someone came to look in on him. This was the way his life had gone lately, he reflected; he was always left waiting, waiting, waiting, fearing the worst.

It didn't stop him sleeping though. When he woke up the curtains had been opened and he could see two older men asleep in beds opposite his. The bed beside him was occupied also, but he could only see a pair of slippered feet beyond the edge of the curtain that had not been fully drawn on one side. A nurse arrived after a while. She smiled at him. He wanted to talk to her, but could not find the right words at first. She could see his obvious frustration.

'Well hello there,' she said. 'It's good to see you're awake. Don't worry, you're fine. A bit of smoke inhalation, that's all. We'll keep you in for another night then let you go home.'

Home. That word again.

'My Grandad?' Jack said.

'Not a bother on him. He was down to see you earlier but you were fast asleep. He didn't want to wake you.'

'Is he in here too?'

'Yes, yes, but he's fine. You were both very lucky. If your brother hadn't been there to save you, I don't know what would have happened.'

Jack knew this was true. He wished Robert was there so he could thank him – so he could say sorry too.

'Can I go see Grandad now?' Jack asked.

'Not just yet. We have you on a drip, but you should be off it soon. I'll come back to you in a while.'

Jack lay back in the bed and tried to relax. He was so relieved that Grandad was okay, but he still had Willie to worry about.

It was impossible to tell if it was morning or evening. There was some light outside but the windows appeared to be tinted a dull brownish grey or else the sky outside was that colour. He must have dozed again, because when he opened his eyes it seemed a little darker outside and a little brighter inside under the glare of white fluorescent strips.

He wasn't sure how long they'd been there. Peadar, Sally and Mrs. Morrison, all with foolish grins on their faces were standing shoulder to shoulder at the foot of his bed.

'Oh you poor love!' Mrs. Morrison said, and she plonked a bag of grapes down on his legs. Jack never really liked grapes very much, but Mrs. Morrison proceeded to take one out of the bag and without any warning she pushed it into Jack's mouth.

'These are good,' she said, 'Aldi, seedless.' She watched as Jack bit into the grape, chewed quickly and dutifully swallowed.

'Thanks Mrs. Morrison,' he said.

Sally came around the side of the bed and placed her hand on his, her eyes big with pity.

'You poor thing Jack – are you okay?'

Jack nodded. He was invigorated by her touch, but also embarrassed at this display of affection from Sally in front of her mother and brother. He was relieved when Peadar pushed in beside him.

'I couldn't believe it Jack! A fire! How did it start?' he asked.

'I think it was those two – you know, Biker and Ugly.'

'Barton and Kelly?'

'Yeah, I saw them out on the street earlier when I was going to bed.'

'Jesus!'

'Language Peadar!' Mrs. Morrison reached across and slapped Peadar on the arm.

'Sorry Mam.' He turned back to Jack. 'I just can't believe they'd go that far – I know they're bad news and all, but...' He shook his head again. 'You could have been killed,' he said.

There was a moment's silence while both of the boys summoned up a mental image of that most extreme outcome.

'It's lucky Robert was there, wasn't it?' Peadar said.

Jack nodded.

'He saved Grandad too,' Jack said. 'Looks like I'll have to be nicer to him from now on.'

'I suppose you will.'

The two boys laughed quietly together until Jack started coughing uncontrollably.

When he had recovered, Jack called Peadar closer so that he could whisper to him.

'I want you to do me a favour,' he said.

'Okay.'

'I want you to get the blanket from the house for me. I need to go back and see Willie one more time before it's too late. The Rising is almost over. They're on the point of giving up I think.'

'But I won't be able to get into the house. There's no one there now.'

'You have to get it Peadar.'

They wracked their brains to think of something.

'When Robert got me out I think I was wrapped up in the blanket. He might know where it is. He might even have it still.'

'Okay, Jack. I'll find Robert.'

'What are you two whispering about?' Sally asked.

'Nothing, nothing at all. Jack is tired, that's all. I think we should head off now,' Peadar said.

'Your brother is right Sally, the poor boy must be worn out.' Mrs. Morrison put down the now half-empty bag of grapes. She'd been eating them throughout the course of her stay. Jack didn't mind too much. He didn't really like grapes. He'd give the rest to Grandad later on.

Chapter 21

Grandad looked very old sleeping in the hospital bed. Jack approached him quietly, studying his set features, imagining that this must be what a dead man looks like. Grandad opened one eye and smiled at him.

'You're up and about I see,' he said.

'I am Grandad. I thought you were sleeping.'

'No, son. Just resting my eyes.'

Jack smiled. Grandad always said that when he fell asleep in front of the telly in the evening.

'Robert saved us both, didn't he?' Jack asked.

'He did.'

'I'm sorry I wasn't nicer to him. I know it must be hard for him.'

'You've nothing to be sorry for. It's been tough for him alright, but Robert knows it's not been easy for you either.'

Grandad moved over in the bed and patted the blankets by his side.

'Sit up beside me Jack.'

Jack climbed up onto the high bed and Grandad shared his pillow with him so that they were sitting side by side. They sat quietly for a while.

'Grandad, you know that tartan blanket that's in my room?'

'Yes, Jack, what about it?'

'Is it special or anything?'

'It is. It belonged to Angela. Remember how I told you how she loved it; how she always had it with her in the months before she died?'

'But did it make her feel better?'

'I think it did. She always had it with her at the end – you know, she was like the way you'd see a toddler with a comfort blanket. When she passed I didn't have the heart to throw it out.'

Jack said nothing. Grandad looked at him.

'You like that blanket, don't you? I see it on your bed in the mornings.'

'Yeah, I like the feel of it.'

'Maybe Angela is looking after you when you have it with you. I never went in for that kind of thing, but she believed in ghosts and people coming back from the other side and all that stuff.'

Grandad smiled at him.

'If you want to, you can keep it. Think of it as a family heirloom.'

'Thanks Grandad.'

Grandad put his arm around his grandson and the two sat there happily in silence.

Just as he was getting sleepy three over-coated figures stumbled into the ward noisily.

'Ah Mick, there you are!' Doyler said loudly, provoking a number of shushes from the other patients.

'We had to come when we heard,' Tommy said.

'Here, look, we brought sweets,' Johnner laughed, 'I hope you're allowed eat them, otherwise we'll have to polish them off ourselves, won't we lads?'

Grandad looked delighted to see his friends and even Johnner seemed to be in good form. They all chewed the sweets with varying degrees of success, Tommy having to remove his dentures at one stage to extract a particularly chewy piece of toffee. Of course they wanted to hear all the grim details of the fire, so Jack told them about Biker and Ugly, or Barton and Kelly as Peadar called them. They were appalled and each vowed that the Guards would be informed as soon as possible. When Jack got to the part where Robert saved the day, they could not say enough kind things about him.

'Sure isn't he an O'Connor lads, so why are we surprised?' Johnner asked.

Everyone nodded. Why indeed?

Jack was pleased to see Grandad and his friends so happy together again.

After a little while the nurse came and scolded them for being too loud and staying beyond visiting time, but Jack could tell that she was not really angry. She seemed to enjoy the exchange of banter and the harmless teasing that went on between them, even if the other patients on the ward were less than impressed. When they'd all finally gone Jack said goodnight to Grandad, hugging him close for a long time before going back to his own ward.

Jack lay on his hard bed in the dark, listening to the night-time sounds of the hospital. The place was never silent. Doors banged and trollies squealed on un-oiled wheels. Footsteps came and went, never seeming to reach a destination, but always passing by. Patients in the beds nearby coughed or groaned or farted. He tried to sleep but every time he shut his eyes he saw Willie's face before him, but he could not speak to him; he knew he could not reach him without the blanket. He prayed that Peadar would somehow manage to get his hands on it. But then what? He had no idea.

A distant door banged, and then another, closer this time. Footsteps approached getting louder as they entered the ward. A figure appeared out of the half-dark at the foot of his bed, tall and imposing. Adrenalin pumped through his body and he was alive and on edge in an instant, ready to spring from the bed and flee at any moment.

'Are you awake? It's me, Jack. It's Robert,' a voice whispered.

'Robert?'

'Yes, your brother. I brought you the blanket you wanted.'

Robert came around to the side of the bed and placed the blanket beside Jack. Jack sat up in the bed and placed his hand on the familiar material.

'Thank you. Thanks Robert for this.'

'Your friend Peadar told me you needed it.'

'Thanks, I do.'

Neither spoke for a moment and the ward continued to make its night noises around them.

'He told me about how you dream, Jack,' Robert said.

Jack could not see Robert's face clearly in the poor light. He wanted to gauge his brother's opinion of the dreams not just from his words but from his expression also.

'And?' Jack asked.

'It's peculiar,' he said, 'and distressing. This boy Willie is going to be killed it seems. Do you think you can do something to stop it happening?'

'I don't know but I need to see him one more time before it's too late. He's my friend. The first real friend I found when I came here.'

He thought then that Robert was going to leave, but instead he sat down on the side of the bed beside Jack.

'I'm... I'm sorry, Robert,' Jack said. 'I'm sorry for the way I've been with you. I didn't mean to make you feel unwelcome.'

'Didn't you?'

Jack thought about it for a moment.

'You're right. I did want you to feel unwelcome. I wanted you to go away and stay away. I didn't want things to change.'

'And now?'

'It's too late. Everything had changed anyway, before you came along. I blamed you, but it wasn't you. It was everything.'

'Your mam being ill I suppose.'

'Yeah, and all the other stuff too. Matt moving out and me coming here. That was hard – I'd never even met Grandad before last week.'

'But you seem very close.'

'Yes. I feel safe when I'm with him.'

Jack shivered. He took the blanket, opened it out and threw it around his shoulders. He pulled it tight across his chest and the tips of his fingers felt the scorched wool where it had been singed by the fire. He kept his fingers on the spot, rubbing the coarseness as if it was an itch he had to scratch.

'You saved my life Robert. And Grandad's.'

'I wouldn't go that far. I just did what anyone else would do if they were there.'

'No, it's more than that. You saved us, even though I didn't want you around.'

'I knew you'd change your mind about me, just like Grandad did. When I was born he didn't want my mam to keep me, so she gave me up for adoption – he told me so himself. But I don't blame him now. I did for a while of course. But he did what he thought was best for his daughter. It was just the way things were back then.'

'You're very kind to us Robert, considering everything.'

'You think so? I don't know. I just want to get to know you all.'

'I wasn't very nice to you, I'm afraid.'

'No, but you had a lot on your plate before I came along. And now there are these dreams of yours.'

'But they're more than dreams, Robert.'

'Peadar said that these dreams are very vivid,' Robert said.

'They're real. It's real, all of it. I've been living through the Rising with Willie.'

'I don't mean to doubt you Jack, but it sounds like trauma to me. That's where the word dream comes from, the German word *traume*.'

'No, no, I'm not imagining it!'

'That's not what I mean Jack. You've just told me yourself about all the upheaval in your life. You must miss your mam and friends in London. All I mean is that sometimes when we're upset we can experience things we wouldn't normally experience.'

'I don't care what you say, I know what I know.'

'I know you do. I'm sorry.'

'I just want to help Willie if I can, but I don't know how.'

'So now you have the blanket and you plan to see him tonight?'

'Yes.'

'And if he dies, what then?'

'I don't know. At least I will have tried.'

Robert's features were still partially hidden even though they were just feet apart, but Jack could see that he was upset.

'Don't do anything stupid Jack, promise me. I've just found you and I don't want to lose you. We have to get to know each other still.'

'We will,' Jack said, and he reached out his hand and touched Robert's arm.

Robert was silent for a moment and Jack could hear his breathing coming and going quickly.

'When I found you on the landing I thought you were dead.' His words came out as a hoarse whisper.

Footsteps came hurrying into the ward then. It was the nurse again and at this late hour she was far less indulgent.

'You can't be here!' she hissed. 'Have you seen the time? How did you get past me at all?'

Robert stood quickly and turned to her.

'I'm done now, sorry. I just needed to see my brother,' he said.

'Don't worry about me Robert. I'll be fine, I promise,' Jack said.

Jack lay back and tried to sleep. His fingers worried the coarse wool of the blanket, seeking out the hardened marks where the fire had done its work.

Chapter 22

Jack felt the familiar nobbled texture graze his fingertips. He opened his eyes. The air was cold and darkness crowded in around him, but in a corner of the room he could discern a dull light emerging from a small, high window.

'It's morning Jack!' Willie whispered.

'But it's so cold,' Jack said.

He shut his eyes again and opened them and even in that instant the room seemed to brighten a little; he could make out the shapes of others lying in makeshift beds and cots around the room. Willie got up swiftly and threw on the coat that recently had served him as a blanket.

'Come on,' he said, 'let's see what's going on down at the GPO.'

Jack rose slowly, watching Willie as he cut some bread and buttered it for their breakfast. He felt guilty for taking food from this poor family, but not enough to stop him from stuffing a hunk of bread into his mouth when Willie offered it. He didn't want to take his eyes off his friend, constantly afraid of what was about to happen. Willie's death was history after all, it was fact. How could he change that?

He noticed a small brown official-looking envelope on the mantelpiece with Willie's name typed on it. It was his last wage packet from the newspaper, empty now of course. He took it when no one was looking, as a keepsake, and stuffed it in his pocket.

Outside on the street they ate the bread hungrily as they hurried past the Four Courts. The streets were quiet still, and they could clearly hear the boom of artillery as it pummelled Sackville Street. Mary Street and Henry Street were nothing more than rutted lanes between ruins and rubble. The heart of the city had been destroyed. Jack watched as Willie surveyed the mess. Like all boys their age he would have loved to poke about among the debris to see what treasure he might find, but he quelled his natural inclination when he saw Willie's sad confusion.

'This was never supposed to happen Jack,' he said, indicating the debris all around them. 'These were people's homes, people worked here. I never thought the British would blow up the city like this.'

'They just want the volunteers to surrender,' Jack said.

'They'll never surrender!' Willie puffed out his chest and held up his chin, but Jack knew that it was just bluster.

'It's only a matter of time now Willie,' Jack said. 'Maybe we should just go home and wait until it's all over.'

Willie stopped and looked at the ground for a while, and for a moment Jack thought he might have gotten through to him.

'Listen!' Willie said. 'They've stopped firing for now. We might get near to the garrison.'

He hurried off and Jack followed him reluctantly.

They could see Nelson on his Pillar through the morning mist and the dust caused by the shelling. It looked like he was floating on air. The GPO was almost entirely ruined. From some distance they could see clearly into the building and blue sky was visible through the roof which had been almost totally destroyed.

The guns started up again suddenly and Jack could have sworn he saw some haggard men cowering in the ruined shell of the building before everything was hidden again by the smoke and dust.

'Let's get out of here,' Jack said, and Willie didn't argue this time. They went back the way they'd come and turned right through the markets. The place was much busier now; it was as if the people knew that the Rising was almost over. Carts were being loaded with fresh fruit and vegetables and men exchanged money and chat, hands thrust in their pockets or clutching pipes or cigarettes as they talked. But all the while in the background there was the distant sound of guns.

The boys made their way along North King Street where the occasional gunshot could be heard.

'We should stay in out of the road,' Jack said, grabbing Willie's sleeve.

Willie wrenched his arm away. He looked angry.

'I'll walk where I like,' he said. 'This is my town!'

'No one's saying it isn't,' Jack said, 'just stay in for God's sake.'

Willie turned to him then. There were tears in his eyes.

'It's all over Jack. It's finished, isn't it?'

The two boys stood in the middle of the road looking at each other. Jack wanted to put his arms around his friend and hug him tight, but he couldn't do it. He wasn't the kind of boy who liked to touch others or be touched. Now he hated himself for his reluctance. He thought about how his friend was going to die, but still he didn't move or reach a hand out to Willie's arm.

A single shot rang out, biting a lump out of the road beside them. Willie did not move, but Jack turned in the direction from which he thought it came. He stood in front of Willie and raised his fist in anger.

'Leave us alone! We're only kids for God's sake!' he shouted.

He shut his eyes and waited. The sniper fired off another round and he felt his heart stop for an instant, but he was not hit.

'Come on Jack, let's get out of here,' Willie said, and he dragged Jack to the side of the road and down a lane away from danger.

They wandered around the city all day, hardly talking at all, trying their best to forget what was going on, trying simply to be kids again for one day. But both were constantly tuned to the distant sounds of gun and cannon fire. They raced each other in the polo grounds in Phoenix Park and walked the perimeter of the zoo looking in vain for a weak spot where they might get access.

After a while Jack got hungry but he knew that Willie's mother had little or no food at home. As they walked back along the quays a soldier from the barracks called them over. Willie was reluctant to go near him, but Jack could see that behind the uniform he was only a young man, not much older than Willie's brother Seán.

'You boys look hungry,' the soldier said.

'We are,' Jack said quickly.

The soldier had a London accent and Jack felt a little ashamed because he was thrilled to hear it.

'Hang on a mo and I'll get something for you.'

He disappeared into the main building for a minute and the two boys looked at each other.

'Come on, we should go home,' Willie said.

'No, wait. Here he is now.'

The two boys watched in amazement as the soldier appeared carrying two huge cheese sandwiches. He smiled broadly at them.

'This should fill a hole,' he said.

'Thanks,' Jack said.

'Yeah, thanks mister,' Willie said.

The two boys started on the sandwiches straight away and the soldier laughed.

'Take it easy lads, or you'll get indigestion!'

'Don't care,' Willie said between mouthfuls.

The soldier laughed again and lit a cigarette. He stood with them for a while and smoked.

It was getting late. The evening was falling and the city along the dark river looked beautiful but sad, Jack thought. Then he noticed something else.

'Listen!' he said.

Willie stopped chewing for a minute.

'I can't hear anything,' he said.

'Exactly. The shelling's stopped.'

'That doesn't mean anything – it stopped before. It always starts again,' Willie said.

'Not this time!' the soldier chipped in. 'It's all over now, thank God.'

'What do you mean?' Jack asked.

'They surrendered an hour ago. It's all over. The leaders have all been arrested.'

Willie looked on the verge of tears. He shook his head as if he didn't want to believe it. He threw the remnants of his sandwich into the gutter. Jack thanked the soldier for the food once again and led Willie up the Quays a bit.

'Are you alright?' Jack asked.

'I think so. I just can't believe it's over. We didn't even see out the week.'

'I'm glad it's over, Willie,' Jack said. 'There'll be no more killing now.'

He placed his hand on Willie's shoulder and Willie tried his best to smile.

'I was worried about you all week,' Jack said, 'but you're safe now.'

'I know. It's just that... what was it all for if we give up now?'

'Trust me Willie, it matters. More than you can know. Let's just go home now.'

Willie wiped a tear away roughly with the sleeve of his jacket.

'I'll walk home with you some of the way Jack,' he said.

The two boys crossed the river as the night fell about them. A lot of the streets were still in darkness as they walked and very few people were abroad.

'Your grandad will be disappointed,' Willie said after a while.

'I suppose,' Jack said.

Their footsteps echoed in the darkness of the empty streets, but in the distance he could hear a noise he thought might be thunder, or heavy barrels being rolled across cobblestones. Even though he didn't recognise the street, he had the sense that he had been this way before. The cool night air breathed in his face and for a moment he thought of his mother. He wondered would he ever see her again; would his life ever be the same again.

'We're almost there,' Jack said. 'You should go on home Willie.'

They rounded the corner and Jack realised that they were now on his grandfather's street. Suddenly there was a scattering of shouts at one end of the street and then a deafening high-pitched sound that seemed to echo off the fronts of the terraced houses – a kind of shrill zinging. The air was filled with the smell of smoke. The boys threw themselves on the ground instinctively. It was just as it had been the first time he met Willie, when he thought that it was just a dream. Jack reached out a hand to feel for Willie but felt only the damp cold stone of the road. He shut his eyes tight and opened them again, but there was only darkness. He heard heavy boots running, coming closer, a momentary pause and then more gunfire.

'Willie!' he shouted. 'Willie, where are you?'

'I'm here!' Willie hissed.

He was taking shelter in the doorway of a house. Jack stood up quickly and ran to join him, but just as he did he heard a volley of shots ring out and he fell onto the cobble stones. He lay there wondering what he should do. He heard the soldiers running footsteps as they left the street pursuing their quarry. He tried to call out for Willie, but he could not make a sound. After a moment Willie's face appeared over him, his eyes full of tears.

'Jack? Jack?' Willie cried and put his hand on Jack's forehead. Jack could feel nothing. He could not answer his friend but he tried to smile up at him.

Willie sat in the road beside him and cried and cried. Jack listened to him for a long time until the sound of his sobbing turned in on itself and became something different, something mechanical and repetitive like a door swinging on a rusty hinge. But soon even that receded and the absence of noise mingled with the absence of light created nothingness. Silence was dark; darkness was silent.

Chapter 23

It was a kind of sleep, he supposed, when he actually thought about it later. It was a shallow, dreamless sleep in which he sensed the close proximity of waking life. But he couldn't go there, even though he could almost taste and smell the living world. When he finally did wake up he did not feel refreshed or rested. Is that what death is like, he wondered. A nurse who was just coming on duty that morning found his inert body at the foot of the main stairs. He was concussed and blood trickled down his left cheek. The duty nurse could not explain how he had got past the nurse's station at the ward, but he had somehow. He had been sleepwalking again, and the CCTV footage confirmed it when an anxious hospital administrator looked at it later that day and saw a small zombie-like boy wrapped in a tartan blanket making his way slowly down empty strip lit corridors.

They put him in a room in ICU on his own and monitored him all day, but still he did not wake. He was oblivious to the line of visitors who came and went: Grandad, Robert, Matt who'd flown in from London the evening before, Mrs. Morrison, Sally and Peadar, Doyler, Tommy and Johnner. They all looked at him laid out in the bed as pale and fragile as a doll, but he was oblivious to all of them.

He did not wake as the sun rose again over the city spreading its light fingers across Ringsend and Irishtown towards the city centre. He did not wake as kids went out to school and men and women made their way to work along the sunlit canal that was a strip of mercury oozing through the core of the city. He did not wake as the buses pulled in on O'Connell Street, or while upstairs commuters looked idly at the GPO, their faces turned away sun-blinded by the glare off Lord Nelson's replacement, the Spire. And he did not wake when the sun broke through a crack in the blinds and crept across the ICU room floor warming his immobile form.

He woke only when Peadar spoke to him. It was the second time he'd visited Jack after the fall, but he had not said a word the first time. He'd simply stood beside his mother as she talked to no one in particular about how unfortunate young Jack had been. She listed all the terrible things that had happened to the boy since he came to Dublin and Peadar began to think that she was right, that maybe Jack was jinxed in some cruel way and this was his predestined fate, to die before he even had a proper life. He knew that his accident had something to do with Willie's fate and he regretted going to Robert to get the blanket for his friend. Without the blanket Jack wouldn't have been able to visit Willie again and he'd be fine now. He cursed the blanket and himself.

The hospital strictly applied the rule that only two people were allowed to visit ICU patients at a time and while his mother spoke to Jack's grandad in the corridor Peadar saw his chance to see Jack on his own. Jack's skin was pale and smooth – it seemed to glow with a grim vigour like the false sheen on the dummies he'd seen in the wax museum. That was it exactly. It was Jack alright, but at the same time it was not. Devoid of animation he was like a pale imitation of his friend, albeit a well-made and skilfully executed copy. His breathing was so slight it hardly registered.

After a moment's hesitation Peadar went over to the bedside and touched Jack's face with his fingertips. Even in such a warm room his skin seemed cold and damp to the touch. Like a dead person's, he thought.

'Jack.' He tried the name out loud and his voice sounded high and breathless in the silence of the room.

'You should have let things be,' he whispered. 'Poor Willie was going to die anyway – there was nothing you could do – and now look what's happened to you.'

Still he did not respond. Peadar exhaled, a long slow breath. He was so close now that Jack's long hair was stirred to life, and even that small quickening gave Peadar a strange impression that Jack was really there. He had an urge to punch him on the shoulder, to rouse him from his supposed sleep as if it was a trick he was playing on his friend that Peadar had grown tired of.

'I thought we'd be friends forever Jack,' he said.

Nothing. He had not really expected a reply.

Behind the vertical blinds the sun was high in the sky. They should have been outside together playing football or strolling along the canal. Not here. Not like this. Small droplets of water fell on Peadar's hands and on the faded green hospital coverlet. He was crying – silently at first, in keeping with the silence all around him – but after a few moments he gave in completely. He didn't care if his mother or Sally saw him. What did anything matter now that his new friend was dead?

'It's okay Willie, I'm okay,' Jack said.

Peadar turned to him, his eyes open wide now in amazement. Jack returned his look, his features blank, but his blue eyes were wide open too.

'Jack! Jack!' Peadar almost pulled him from the bed. 'You're okay, you're still alive!'

'Peadar?' Jack asked.

'Yes, it's me Jack. What?'

'I thought you were Willie,' was all he said.

For a moment Peadar's joy was crushed. He thought of Jack's other, phantom friend; he imagined poor Willie dead somewhere in another time, in another place.

'He didn't die, Peadar.'

Peadar was not sure what to say. Jack was obviously delirious from the concussion still. After all Willie's name was on a plaque along with others at the exhibition in the museum.

'*Sssh* Jack! You should get some rest. You got a bad bang on the head.'

Just as he said this the door opened and Grandad walked in. For an awful moment Peadar thought the shock of seeing his grandson awake again was going to be too much for him. He pictured himself running up and down the corridors of the hospital looking for a doctor for the old man. But he didn't need to worry. Grandad, after a slight hesitation in which he almost lost his balance, gave out a shout of happiness.

'Jack! Jack my lad!' His eyes filled with tears as threw his arms around the boy.

'Grandad. I missed you, Grandad,' was all Jack said.

'I know. I missed you too.'

Grandad was sobbing quietly now as he held his grandson, and Jack closed his eyes and breathed in the now familiar smell of his grandfather. It felt like home.

'Are you okay son?' Grandad asked.
'I'm fine now Grandad, I'm absolutely fine.'

Chapter 24

That evening they moved him back to a shared ward. The doctors advised that he remain there for another day or so for observation because of the severity of his concussion. He woke the following morning with a strange feeling in the pit of his stomach and the tartan blanket wrapped around his shoulders. He could not name this feeling, but the best guess he could make was that it was regret, or something like it. For the first time the blanket had not worked; he had not visited Willie in the past. He understood that, from then on, the blanket would be just like any other blanket. But it did not stop him thinking about Willie and what he might have done with the life he managed to hold on to in spite of history.

It was early and no light cut through the broken blinds just yet. The room was like the other ward he'd been in, shared with many other patients, and though he could not see them he could hear them shuffle and cough and mutter under their breaths. He was reminded of the tenement rooms he'd slept in with Willie, except that here in the hospital the air was far too hot and dry. Outside in the corridors he could hear the clanking of trolleys being wheeled around bringing breakfast at an ungodly hour to the sick and sleepless. Light from the corridor spilled into the ward and the woman with the trolley bounded in with a clank and a crash, waking the few lucky patients who had managed to remain asleep. She'd obviously been up for hours and did not heed a normal person's waking or eating routines. Hospital time was different to real time, Jack could see.

After breakfast he dozed a little but could not really sleep. He had numerous truncated dreams. In one he was playing football for the school and the coach replaced him before it even got to half time. He was so upset he couldn't speak. Tears burned his eyes and he felt very young and all alone. In another, his mother was with him and they were walking by a river in the countryside. She was holding his hand as they walked. She told him that she would always be with him no matter what. He woke with the sound of her voice in his ears as real as if she were there beside him in the ward. He turned on his side with his face to the window and cried quietly.

He must have dozed again after a while because when he woke the sunlight from outside filled the room. The door of the ward burst open and in marched a line of people all calling his name and smiling: Grandad, Robert, Matt, Peadar, Tommy, Doyler and Johnner. He sat up in bed, smiling, surprised by how happy he was to see these people, most of whom he did not know two weeks before. One by one they brought him gifts of grapes (from Grandad), sweets (from Peadar), a football magazine (from Matt), a book about the Rising (from Robert), and a Dublin football jersey from Tommy, Doyler and Johnner.

There was an awkward silence for a moment with so many people around his bed. Grandad sat up beside Jack and put his arm around him. Matt smiled at him.

'You've had some adventures I believe,' he said.

Jack looked perplexed and then a little anxious.

'I don't know what you mean...' he began.

'I told them, Jack,' Peadar said. 'I told them all about your dreams, about Willie and the Rising.'

Jack frowned at him.

'There's no harm in it,' Grandad said taking up the tartan blanket that lay on a chair beside the bed. 'So this is what took you back?'

'Yes,' Jack said. 'Anytime I slept with it, but if I didn't have it I didn't go back there.'

'I told you Angela believed it had certain powers – it used to ease her pain before she died. It belonged to an aunt of hers, a woman she was very fond of. She gave it to us as a wedding gift. I remember at the time saying something disparaging about it to Angela, about how stingy I thought the woman was only giving us an oul' blanket, and Angela was really hurt. But that was before I saw what it could do.'

'Is it magic?' Tommy asked.

'Don't be stupid!' Johnner quipped, laughing.

'Don't laugh Johnner,' Grandad said, 'it mightn't be magic but there's something about it alright.'

Jack thought it seemed funny to hear Grandad talking like this in front of so many people.

'And the young fella you met in your dream – Willie, was it?' Grandad asked.

'Yes, Willie Mahon.'

'And this Willie, he wasn't killed? You told Peadar,' Grandad said.

Peadar looked at Jack and showed him the palms of his hands and raised his eyebrows by way of apology.

'But his name is on the list of the children who were killed during Easter week,' Grandad went on. 'We went down to the museum again, didn't we lads?' He looked around the bedside at Tommy, Doyler and Johnner. All three nodded. 'His name is definitely down there as dead.'

'But he didn't die, Grandad,' Jack said looking up at the old man. 'The bullet hit me instead.'

'In your dream,' Grandad said kindly.

'It wasn't a dream, Grandad! Willie is as real as you are now.'

'I know son.' He smiled at Jack. 'So you were shot instead of Willie, but you're okay now?' Grandad rubbed Jack's arm and tightened his hold on his grandson.

'I'm grand, Grandad,' Jack said, smiling.

'You sound really Irish there Jack, the way you said that,' Peadar said.

'I am Irish, Peadar. I just never realised it really until I came here.'

Grandad's three pals gave a spontaneous cheer that prompted a cross nurse to put her head around the door and shush them loudly.

'God, she's awful rude!' Tommy said.

'Can you tell us about the dreams Jack? About young Willie Mahon?' Johnner asked.

'Not now lads, maybe later, poor Jack has been through a lot,' Robert cut in.

'I was thinking maybe we could try and find out what happened to him and his family,' Johnner said, looking at Doyler and Tommy. 'We've got some time on our hands and the library has loads of info on stuff like this. Everyone's checking out their family history nowadays.'

'Yeah, that sounds good to me,' Doyler said.

'We'll report back to you when we get some news,' Tommy said.

All three seemed pleased with each other. They whispered animatedly among themselves. Matt and Robert exchanged a few words and briefly shook hands. Peadar was standing beside the bed on the far side of Grandad. He just stared at Jack all the while, a permanent smile on his face.

'Can I go home, Grandad?' Jack asked.

'It won't be long now,' Grandad said quietly.

Jack thought he heard a note of sadness in his voice and he was upset. He wondered was there bad news about his mother. He had to ask Matt; he needed to know the truth.

'Is Mum better Matt?'

'We'll get the test results some time tomorrow,' Matt said, 'but the doctors say the signs look good. You'll be able to see her soon.'

Jack could tell that all the others were looking at him now to see what he would do or say. The good news about his mum made him happy, but he found he could not smile. He looked at Grandad, and Grandad tried his best to smile at him but all Jack could see was a tired sadness in his eyes. The others began to talk again among themselves, to fill the silence that had grown around the old man and his grandson and soon they began to leave in ones and twos. Finally Grandad said goodbye, kissing his grandson on the cheek so that Jack could feel the reassuring burn of the old man's wiry bristles on his face.

'Goodbye Jack,' he said. 'Peadar, I'll wait for you downstairs. Don't be too long. Jack needs his rest.'

The two friends were quiet for a moment.

'I'm sorry Jack but I had to tell them about Willie,' Peadar said.

'Maybe it's just as well you did,' Jack said. 'They probably think I'm nuts!'

'No they don't Jack.' He laughed. 'Well maybe just a little bit!'

The boys laughed together for a while and then were silent. Jack looked out the window and saw a huge white seagull on a roof across the way. For the first time he noticed how big and sharp their beaks were and how pure and white their feathers were, so smooth they seemed to have the texture of well-groomed fur.

Peadar turned to him smiling.

'Even Johnner's gone soft on you,' he said.

Jack smiled at his friend and then grew serious again.

'I know why they think it was Willie who died,' he said.

Jack thought Peadar was about to say something, but he didn't.

'I had his wage envelope in my pocket when I got shot. When they found my body they must have assumed I was Willie Mahon – why would someone be carrying another boy's wage packet?'

'It's hard to think about that,' Peadar said. 'About you dying.'

Jack nodded. 'I know,' he said, 'but it's better than thinking of poor Willie dying. After all, I'm still here, aren't I?'

'You are alright,' Peadar said. 'And you're not going anywhere either! Now get some rest.' He smiled at his friend and walked to the door, turning briefly to wave goodbye.

Jack looked around at the men in the ward. None of them looked very well. He hated illness. It was so unfair. He watched the last of their visitors make their way home, politely harried by the ward Sister. Then he looked at each of the men who remained one by one and wondered what they were suffering from. He hoped they would recover and go back to the lives they had before. He knew that some of them wouldn't make it home at all, or if they did, then it would be only for a period of time after which they would be admitted once again, a little older this time, a little frailer. Hospital isn't like the real world either, he knew. It's like a place where things get confused and people get forgotten. He thought of his mother then and wished that she would be well again. It was a kind of prayer, he thought.

Later that evening when he was dozing, when the bright strip lights had been extinguished and the only light was the dull yellow glow that seeped in through the crack in the ward door and the red and blue pulse of the machines that helped monitor the hearts and organs of the sick men all around him, Jack fell into a dream.

He walked for the last time through the rubble and destruction of the city, but this time he didn't meet Willie. In fact, nobody saw him or acknowledged him at all. He was a ghost. He wandered past kids scouring the rubble of shops and old men smoking pipes and discussing the Rising. There was no sympathy there for the leaders who had been arrested. One man in the group spat on the ground and cursed the others for speaking the way they did. But he was just one among many, and he went off on his own very soon.

He wandered up Henry Street, past the Four Courts and into Cuckoo Lane hoping to run into Willie. He waited outside the tenement for what seemed like ages but he saw no one he knew. He realised now that this was not like before, that this was just a dream. He sat down on the cobbles and brought his knees up to his chest and slept for a while.

When he woke, the light streamed in through a crack high up in the blinds and the lady with the breakfast trolley had already been. He looked up and Robert was standing at the foot of the bed.

'You'll be getting out today,' he said.

'I hope so. I can't wait to be home with Grandad again.'

'I came in early to see you because I'm going away.'

'But why? Is it because of me, Robert?'

Robert laughed softly.

'No, no Jack, don't be silly. I just need to get a job that's all. I was hoping I'd get something in Dublin but that hasn't happened. No, I'm going to London to see how I get on.'

'To London? That's great! We can meet up when I get back home. We can go and see Arsenal with Matt.'

'That would be great. I'd like that.'

The two brothers looked at each other for a moment and smiled.

'Well, I better get going,' Robert said. 'I shouldn't be here at all really, only the nurse there was very nice.'

Just then she appeared in the doorway and motioned to Robert to make tracks. She was small and blonde and very pretty. Jack had not seen her before.

Robert reddened a little. He moved awkwardly around to the side of Jack's bed and leaned in and gave him a hug.

'Goodbye little brother. I'll be seeing you soon.'

'Goodbye Robert.'

Robert hurried out without looking back.

Epilogue

It was the evening of a glorious day in late May, a month after Jack returned to London. He was sitting at an outside table in an Italian restaurant on Upper Street in Islington with his mum and Matt. Matt poured white wine into his mum's glass and as he did so Jack watched their faces closely, satisfied that they were happy together now. When the waiter arrived with a notebook to take their order Matt told him that they were waiting for another person to arrive.

Robert had been in touch regularly with Jack and his mum by phone but this was to be only the second time they actually met since he came to London. The first time Robert visited, Matt took Jack to the cinema, and when they came home they found Mum and Robert sitting together smiling but red-eyed, in the living room. Robert had done well for himself in London. He found a job at a university library and was already making plans to continue his studies at night the following year. He lived in Canning Town in the East End with a new friend he had made through work and he genuinely seemed happy. Jack truly hoped he was. He deserved it. Tonight was going to be an important night for all of them, but mostly for Robert and Jack's mum because it would be the first time they would all go out together as a family.

The sun sank completely behind the buildings and still there was no sign of Robert. The streetlights came on giving the twilight a golden tinge, and the hubbub of conversation and the noise of traffic from the street mingled, adding to the air of excitement and expectation. Jack had chosen the pizza he wanted from the menu within minutes of taking his seat and now his stomach growled. Where on earth was Robert?

'How did football go then?' Mum asked.

'I made the squad, but I think I'll start as sub for the next game.'

'That's great news,' Matt said. 'Be sure to let me know when it's on and I'll try to sneak away from work for it.'

'I just wish I made the first eleven.'

'You've been away Jack – you've done really well to get picked at all,' Mum said, placing her hand on his.

There was a time, up to quite recently, when he would have quickly removed his hand and groaned audibly when she did this, but not anymore.

'Is Grandad coming over soon?' he asked.

'It will be July before he gets here, but it's better that way. School will be over and we'll all have lots of time to show him around.'

Mum turned in her seat so that she was facing Jack.

'I'm really glad you two got on so well,' she said.

'Grandad's great,' Jack said. He became animated suddenly. 'At last! Here's Robert!'

Robert was hurrying along the crowded pavement with a large envelope in his hand. He was over-dressed for the weather in a blue sweater and jacket and his face was red, as if he'd been running. He was almost out of breath when he arrived. He shook Matt's hand and Jack stood up and hugged him.

'I thought you'd never come Robert,' he said, 'I'm starving here!'

They all laughed and there was a slight hesitation while Mum stood up to greet him. It was awkward because the table and the chairs were in the way, but Mum stepped calmly to the side and put her arms around Robert without saying a word. Jack was struck by how alike they were. He hadn't seen it before, but looking at them now there was no doubting they were mother and son.

'Oh Robert,' she said. 'I can't tell you how happy this makes me.'

'And me,' Robert said shyly.

They just stood there looking at each other, holding hands for a long time, as if they were looking in a mirror, Jack thought.

'Sit down, sit down,' Matt said. 'Let's order – like Jack says, I'm absolutely starving!'

'I'm sorry for being so late,' Robert said, 'but I got a call from Mick – er, Grandad – just before I left work. Then his pals sent me an email and I had to print all this stuff off. He was very excited!'

'How is he? We were just talking about him,' Matt said.

'Oh he's fine; he's looking forward to his visit during the summer.'

'But what did he want?' Jack asked.

Robert placed the large envelope on the table in front of him and smiled at Jack.

'Johnner and Doyler and Tommy were as good as their word,' Robert said.

'Hold on, I'm lost here,' Mum said.

'Grandad's friends,' Matt said, 'they were going to do a little research on this Willie Mahon fellow and his family.'

'Who's Willie Mahon?' Mum asked.

Robert and Matt both looked at Jack then.

'You mean you didn't tell her?' Matt said.

'Didn't tell me what?'

Mum turned to Jack then, her head tilted to one side like she does when she's scolding or asking a question that there's no right answer to.

'I didn't want to bother you, Mum,' Jack said.

'Well, you can bother me now then.'

So Jack had to go back to the start and tell his mum all about those first nights at Grandad's place and the tartan blanket and the meetings with Willie in 1916. Mum remembered the blanket and how her mother could not be separated from it in the months before she died. Tears filled her eyes and Jack felt bad for making her feel sad, but she said no, she wasn't sad at all. She was happy, she said, although Jack thought that crying was a funny way to show it. But then again, adults sometimes did the strangest things. Mum said she wanted to hear more about Jack's adventures. So he talked and talked as they ate and as he told the story it seemed to him that it all happened a long time ago. And it did, he supposed, for Willie. When he finished Robert opened the envelope and took out what looked like photocopies of some official looking papers.

'The lads started in their local library with the census of 1911,' he said spreading out some documents on the table. 'Somehow they ended up making contact with a woman called Millie Hansard in Chicago, Illinois.'

Robert looked around the table at the others, a huge smile on his face, waiting for the questions to come.

'So who is this Millie person?' Mum asked.

'She is the granddaughter of William Mahon,' Robert declared.

Nobody said anything for a moment. Jack's mind raced to establish the implications of Robert's statement. If she was Willie's granddaughter then that meant that Willie had a child which meant that Willie really did survive the Rising and the exhibition was wrong to put him on the list of casualties.

'So the historians got it wrong then?' Matt asked.

'It certainly looks that way,' Robert grinned. 'This woman is living proof of their mistake.' He tapped the documents on the table in front of him with his index finger.

'So let me get this straight,' Mum said, leaning in across the table and lowering her voice. 'You're telling me that this boy, this Willie Mahon, was listed as killed in the Rising and now my father's friends have proved that he did in fact survive.'

'That's right,' Robert said. 'And it was Jack here who saved him!'

'But surely, there's some mistake,' she began.

'No, it's all here,' Robert said. 'The whole family upped sticks after the Rising and moved to America. They ended up in Chicago and Willie got married there.' He looked through his notes for a moment. 'Let me see, he had three kids, Mary, Bridget and one son called Jack.'

All eyes turned to Jack then. Willie had named his son after him. Robert went on.

'Mary never married, but Bridget and Jack did, and Jack had a daughter called Millie.' Robert took a photo of a sixty something year old woman form the envelope and laid it on the table. The woman was small and neatly dressed in navy slacks and a blue and white sweater. Her short hair was flecked with grey. She was smiling. Jack studied the photo looking for some vestige of Willie as he remembered him but he found nothing.

Robert reached into the envelope again and he produced another photograph. This time it was a black and white wedding photo, a young man and his bride smiling arm in arm.

'It's him! It's him! It's Willie!' Jack stood up. 'I knew he'd be alright! I knew he'd make it!'

The others looked at the photo more closely; a young lad in his early twenties holding the arm of the girl that he loved, and both of them smiling happily into the camera, seeing only a bright future ahead. On the bottom left corner were written the words: *Willie and Nora, Oakland, March 28th 1928.*

Jack sat back down in his seat. The others were silent. He looked at his mother and noticed how she'd aged over the course of the past few weeks. He had a sense of time passing him by. But he was not afraid anymore. He vowed to do everything he could from now on to help her. And he thought about Willie and his family and all that they had to go through and he promised himself that he would never again be afraid for himself or his future.

Ends

About the Author

Brian Kirk is an award winning poet and short story writer from Dublin. He was shortlisted for Hennessy New Irish Writer Awards for fiction in 2008 and 2011.

His maternal Grandfather was a member of the Royal Irish Constabulary (RIC) while his Grand Aunt was quartermaster for Cumann na mBan during 1916. Consequently he tries to have a balanced view of history.

He blogs at: http://briankirkwriter.com/